Jenna's Gang of Deadheads

by

Paul Atreides

World of Deadheads Series

Jenna's Gang of Deadheads

Cover Art by *Debbie Taylor*

The Wild Rose Press, Inc.
PO Box 708
Adams Basin, NY 14410-0708
Visit us at www.thewildrosepress.com

Publishing History
First Mainstream Fantasy Edition, 2017
Print ISBN 978-1-5092-1280-4
Digital ISBN 978-1-5092-1281-1

World of Deadheads Series
Published in the United States of America

Even though the sun blared down
on the group of mourners, it was a calm, cold day. Not a wisp of wind added to the chill factor. David still made short but sweet work of a eulogy. When Mr. Davis held out the ceremonial shovel, David took it, and walked to JoAnne. "Here, we'll do this together."

Jenna stepped to the mound of dirt that would fill in her grave. She grabbed a handful and tossed it in before a startled "No!" burst from the crowd of deadheads who'd gathered.

A gasp rose from the living. Some gaped around in fright and backed away. Madelyn let loose with a piercing shriek, clutched her husband's arm with both hands in a death grip. "Holy Mother of Mary! Morton, what the hell was that?"

"Ow!" Morton yanked his arm free. "It had to be a gust of wind."

"What? What did I do?" Jenna gaped around the crowd of deadheads for an answer. Though Madelyn's outburst sure explained where Marvin had gotten his favorite turn of phrase when something took him by surprise.

"You just scared the crap out of everyone. You have to time it, Jen," Marv admonished, and laughed along with the rest of the dead, who now found his mother's reaction quite humorous. "You wait for them to toss a shovelful and throw yours at the same time."

Mike waved him off. "Oh, Brody, give her a break. She's still new around here. She'll catch on."

"Yeah, besides, Marvin," Tommy offered, "maybe it woke some people up."

"Are you saying my brother delivered a boring eulogy? Is that what you're saying, hippie?"

Dedication

Dedicated to fans of the afterlife and ghostly fun.
And to the multitude of people who work tirelessly
to help victims of domestic violence and abuse;
you have my sincere gratitude.

Chapter 1

"See? See? What did I tell you?" Marvin Broudstein jumped from the booth in Epstein's Deli, his favorite eatery near downtown Dayton, Ohio. He whirled around, his arms outstretched to include all the deadheads (as he had dubbed them shortly after he'd died, with sincere apologies to Grateful Dead groupies). Most had gotten used to his outbursts over the past months and ignored him as they lingered over coffee, or the bagel they'd snagged from the case.

"What? Dude, all she did was ask a simple question," Tommy Sinclair said from the opposite side of the table where he sat next to Mike.

"Bullshit!" Marvin accused from his position behind the bench of the booth next to the window; the one he'd insisted on occupying since he grew weary of the waitress, "Tina-I'll-Be-Your-Server-Today," pushing and adjusting tables and chairs in some mad rush to keep up with the crowds of patrons. Well, the paying ones, anyway.

Of course, being alive and breathing, Tina couldn't see the dead folks to know they were there and the chairs went right through them if they didn't manage to scramble out of her way. It was the same booth where the group gathered each mid-morning for coffee, in the deli where Tommy had worked as a short-order cook before he'd been gunned down during a robbery-gone-bad in late 1969. On Sunday mornings, when the place was closed, they sat in comfort and leisure while Tommy fired up the grill to cook for a crowd of deadheads.

But, on this particular weekday morning they sat safely out of the reach of Tina's slamming chairs, and Marvin pointed at the back of Jenna's head. "She always accused me of trying to postpone the wedding and now look who's hedging—again!"

"Marv, come on. All I asked was—" Jenna paused for a new tactic. "I mean, the vows can't be "until death do us part," we're dead already. And who's going to care now whether we're married or not?"

"That's not the point and you know it!" Marvin poked a finger into her back to emphasize his point.

Jenna swatted him away as blithely as she would a fly that had landed on her coffee cup. "Eternity is a long time, Marvin. I've only been here for few days and you're ranting about our wedding already."

"Oh, here we go with the excuses again, huh?" Marvin wasn't going to be dissuaded in such an off-handed manner.

"Come on, Brody, sit down." Mike Hamilton pointed to the vacant seat next to Jenna. In college, he'd shortened Marvin's last name of Broudstein to 'Brody.' Not long after, Mike had died in a commuter plane crash in Buffalo, New York, one week after "Sully" Sullenburger safely landed a jetliner in the Hudson River. He sometimes wondered why his pilots couldn't have been as talented. The two college friends reconnected when Mike attended Marvin's funeral. "You're making a spectacle of yourself."

"You know you can be a petulant bitch

sometimes," Marvin grumbled at Jenna, but returned to his seat.

"And you can be an arrogant prick," Jenna said pointedly.

Marvin peered at her out of the corner of his eye. "Oh…go fall down a flight of stairs."

"Go step in front of a bus." Jenna jabbed at him with an elbow so hard it drove through his ribs.

Marvin and Jenna looked at one another and grinned. The verbal sparring had been one of the things they'd both missed after Marvin's death eighteen months earlier. Then, a few days ago, she died in a freak accident tumbling down the stairs of their condo building in a tangle of limbs with her friend and neighbor, Mrs. McClaskey. And the arguments resumed as if they'd never been apart.

"Marvin, dude, people started shacking up years ago. Shit, the commune I grew up on, no one was married. It was all cool, man," Tommy said.

Marvin picked up his coffee cup and it winked out of sight of the living just before Tina-I'll-Be-Your-Server-Today reached to yank it off the table. She stopped short and the breath caught in her throat. She turned to bus other tables while muttering quietly to the amusement of the unseen diners, "Jesus H. Christ! I am not going nuts. I need the job, but I don't know how much longer… No. It's better not to think about it, Tina. Just let it go. Let it go."

Marvin understood where Tommy was trying to go with his comments. He hoisted his cup across the table toward him. "Look hippie, I know you want Jenna to like you, and I've appreciated everything you've done for me since I bit the pavement, but we don't need you to play the middle like that. Besides, I've told you before, we aren't living on a commune. That '60s crap ended a long time ago."

Mike tapped Marv's forearm. "And, as *I* keep pointing out to *you,* Brody, we don't exactly "live" anywhere, now do we?"

Ignoring the remarks, Tommy fixed a mischievous grin on Jenna, one they all knew could lead to trouble. He held up a stop-sign hand to halt Jenna's argument. "But, it could be a real gas. Just think about it. A huge, fancy wedding—and you know the place would be packed!—the dress of your dreams and it won't cost you a dime." He looked to Marvin and Mike for help.

Jenna pushed his hand away. "You know, Tommy, that silly grin may have worked with these two," she said jutting her chin out to indicate both Marvin and Mike, "but it won't go anywhere with me."

"Oh, come on Jenna. It'll be fun. I promise. And we can get Davy to help. You know this kind of thing is right up his alley. Didn't he pick out a fabulous gown for your funeral?"

Marvin waggled his brows. "It is a hot one, all right."

Jenna turned her head toward Marv to glare him down.

"You've got to admit that," Mike said.

"Yeah, Mike, it is pretty," Jenna agreed. "But—"

"Please, Jenna? Please?" Tommy replaced his grin with a pleading, yet hopeful expression.

She heaved a sigh and waved a hand through the air. "I'm tired of the fight."

Tommy's face broke out into a big victory smile. "Cool! I'll talk to Davy this afternoon during the visitation."

"He'll be there?" Jenna's face scrunched into disbelief. "Why?"

"Well, because he dressed you for one thing—"

"Everyone will be there, kiddo," Marvin butted in. "I told you, I couldn't believe it when I walked into my funeral. Wall to wall, and I didn't know anyone but Mike, Davy, and this nutcase here." He pointed to Tommy.

"Speaking of that, I need to get myself ready. If I have to enter the room like some debutante at her coming-out ball I've got a lot of work to do. What time is it?"

It was only when dealing with the living that the dead ever needed to worry about time, and Mike glanced at the ever-present watch on his wrist. "Going on eleven-thirty."

Jenna drained her cup, set it on the table, went to slide out of the booth and bumped halfway through Marvin before the strange melding of molecules buzzed between them, and she stopped. "Come on, Marv, get up. Let me out."

Marvin didn't budge. "You still didn't give me an answer. A wave of the hand is not a 'yes.'"

"I'll think about it. Now, come on, get out of my way." She waited all of two seconds, then rammed right through him and headed for the door. Phantom laughter rolled around the diner as she walked through the front of the building and headed home.

One of the mid-morning regulars (dead, of course) of Epstein's whistled. "Wow. That's one feisty woman you have there, Broudstein."

Marvin graced the guy at the table across the aisle

with a broad, genuine smile. "Yep, she is, isn't she? And, she's learned fast how to maneuver in this world." Marvin returned his attention to his pals, and added, "But, she seems to learn everything fast."

"Dudes, we probably should head out too." Tommy turned to Mike. "The bus should hit our stop in less than ten minutes. By the time we get to the hotel suite and change, we'll barely have enough time to get over to the funeral home."

Marvin and Mike drained their cups and handed them off to Tommy. As Tina began a visual sweep of the empty tables, the cup Jenna had left disappeared from sight. Tina stopped, closed her eyes and counted to ten amid a long, low growl. Tommy moved his way through the diner, waited for Tina to open her eyes, and then he dropped the dirty cups into the bus tray at the waiter's station with a clatter. She let out a frightened yelp and ran to the Ladies room.

The guffaws of the remaining deadheads echoed behind them as they made their way out to the street.

Chapter 2

As the head of the North American Council of Keepers, Jason watched the scuffle unfold from the far end of the alley, ready to take the man the instant he stood from his dead body. Before the attack could play out, Jenna—her face twisted in fury—charged along the narrow pathway and startled Jason. In the time it took him to turn and signal to his protégé, Nancy, for help, Jenna lunged for the gun that was pointed at a cowered victim.

The assailant hesitated, loosed a bark of pain, and grabbed at his forearm. Confusion flickered across his expression at his now-empty hand before he turned his attention back to his young female victim. He backhanded her across the face. "You dare question me? I'll show you. I don't need any gun to shut you up, bitch! I'll just knock the teeth right out of your mouth. Maybe then you'll learn to show me some respect."

Jason came down the alley, his already imposing stature increasing in size with each yard of distance; the darkness within him reaching out in its seething, tumultuous pain and hunger. That someone so new to the world of the dead would need to be punished saddened him, yet he couldn't allow himself to be distracted from his immediate task. He called out to stop the interloper, this woman who dared involve herself in his work. His voice boomed, "Jenna

Wilson…"

Jenna turned at the sound of her name, froze for an instant, threw the gun and ran.

As much as he wanted to go after her, Jason had to stay. As head of the Keepers, the evil he'd come to envelop in the prison of his body was a far greater danger in the world than the one who'd just fled. He turned and waited for the event to unfold, ready to devour the man, but the beating only continued.

The woman ducked a punch, and the man's fist pounded into the concrete wall. Asphalt cinders embedded into the woman's palms as she scrambled on her knees to escape while he stood howling in pain. Then she regained her feet and ran toward the street, gasping and screaming for help between sobs.

Jason scanned the asphalt for the gun that should have provided the woman her ultimate freedom, it hit the ground and spun away, but he thought sure it had remained within reach. He moved toward the young man, expecting he'd been quick enough to recover the weapon and perhaps stuffed it into the waistband of his jeans. Jason splayed his hands in confusion, turned in the direction the young victim had run, shook his head, and his body returned to normal.

Nancy spoke in a soft voice. "It's here. I have it."

"What? No. You can't do that."

"If I hadn't picked it up, he would've killed her." A visible tremble coursed through Nancy's body.

Jason frowned. "No. It was he who would've died."

"How? How could he have ended up being the victim?"

"Why do you think we were here?" Jason scowled

at his student. "I can see you still have a lot to learn before I'm able to shed my burden and find peace."

"I don't understand. They both lived. That's a good thing, isn't it?"

"Evil on that plane is as bad as it is on ours. Do you think he'll stop now that he has no gun? We do not interfere."

"I simply thought—"

"I can understand that young Jenna wouldn't be aware, though she appears to be as headstrong as Marvin had been when I needed to stop him from killing her. But, you? You know the rules, you should not have touched the gun." Jason's anger rose with each word and his body again expanded in height to tower above Nancy. "Had neither of you broken into the encounter, the young woman would've gotten control of the gun, her assailant would be dead and safe within me, where he could do no more harm and become aware of his sins."

Nancy took a step back, but her eyes never left his. "I'm sorry. After Jenna knocked the gun from his grip, I feared for the woman's safety."

"We do not interfere!" Jason repeated. He turned his eyes to the street where Jenna had run. Standing silent for a moment, his anger dissipated, he began to walk and his stature lessened.

Nancy trailed after him. "What do we do now?"

"You will dispose of the gun. I'm going to handle Ms. Wilson."

"What do you mean 'handle'."

Where the alley began at the street, he stopped but didn't turn to face her. "What would you have me do?"

"This was her first offense. How many times did I

see you watch over Marvin's attempts to kill Jenna, only to chuckle and shake your head, and issue a soft word of warning?"

"His assaults were lame, laughable. In the end, I gave him too much latitude. But, in her, I could feel the menace. Her intent was clear."

"But you stopped her."

He looked down at Nancy. "And, so, this dismisses her infraction?"

"No, but…"

Jason turned to the right and continued walking in the direction Jenna had taken. "I cannot allow her to interfere."

"Won't you at least consider an alternative?" His step faltered, and she ran to catch up. "At least give her the chance to learn. Let me talk to her."

"When?"

"Today." Nancy paused. "At the cemetery."

To this considered tactic, Jason replied, "And should you fail?"

"I won't."

Jason stared at her.

Nancy shrugged. "You'll be there."

Chapter 3

"Come on, come on. Where the hell are you?" Marvin paced through the living room waiting for Jenna. He'd already showered and changed into the Armani suit Davy chose for him. He glanced at the clock on his way through the kitchen to the balcony at the front of the building.

Overlooking the street, he peered out in both directions in search of Jenna. He avoided looking down at the pavement so he wouldn't see the spot where he'd died, even though he knew the dark stain of blood had to be a figment of his imagination after all this time. "Shit! It's going on one already. With the amount of time it takes you to get ready…"

A flash of auburn hair, a couple blocks away, caught his attention. When he realized he couldn't see through the woman like he could deadheads, who were just slightly transparent, he figured it couldn't be Jenna. Anxiety rose into his chest. To avoid going off on one of his 'infamous rants,' as Jenna called them—those times when he started complaining about something, where his volume would increase, and there was nothing for it but to let him run his course, or give him a smack upside the head to stop him—he went across the hall to the McClaskey's.

Ignoring the resultant buzz that reminded him of touching a nine-volt battery to his tongue, Marvin stuck his head through the door. "Colleen? Patrick?"

Patrick's voice carried from their dining room. "Marvin, come in! We're just sitting down to a cuppa if you'd like to join us."

They both turned as Marvin rushed through the archway from the living room.

"How are you? You seem a little frazzled." Colleen gestured to the chair across from her, since Patrick had reclaimed his place at the head of the table now that his wife had joined him in death. "Have a seat, dear. A nice cup of tea does wonders for the nerves."

"Thank you." Sitting was the last thing Marvin wanted. Moving would've allowed him to expend his nervous energy, but he needed to mind his manners—Mrs. McClaskey could be a real stickler for those. Because, the *real* last thing he needed was for Jenna to hear about it and think he'd stepped out of line, or been rude to Colleen. He'd never hear the end of it. Jenna had become fast friends with the old woman after Marvin's death and considered their neighbor to be the sweetest person she'd ever encountered.

"You look awfully spruced up," Patrick said, passing the cup of hot tea Colleen held out.

Marvin took a glance at his black coat sleeves and nodded. "You like it? Davy picked it out for me to wear today."

"Who's Davy?"

"Oh, you remember, Patrick," Colleen reminded, sliding a steaming cup across the linen cloth she'd put on the table. "The young man at Nordstrom Jenna recommended we see if we needed new clothes."

"Oh, right, right."

Marvin saw his chance and grabbed it. "You

haven't seen her, have you? Jenna, I mean."

Colleen paused in the preparation of her own tea. "Why, no dear. Why do you ask?"

"She left Epstein's before I did, well over an hour ago, to get ready for her funeral. She still hasn't gotten home."

"That's what's got your nerves on edge, is it? Well, our Jenna is a strong girl though, isn't she? She'll be along, I'm sure of it."

"Oh, I'm not worried she's in trouble. Though she's *gonna* be in trouble, if you know what I mean, if she doesn't get a move on." Marv shook a fist in the air.

Colleen laughed with a little wave of her hand. "Oh, go on!"

"Well, I hate being late," Marvin explained.

"What time does visitation begin, again?" Patrick stirred milk into his tea.

"Two. But, Davy said we should get there at two-thirty." Marv grinned. "You know, he takes quite a bit of pride in what he does and likes to announce the arrival of his clients. And when you get a look at Jen, you'll understand why. You are going, aren't you?"

Patrick cleared his throat, and took a sip of tea.

"Well, of course, we are, aren't we dear?" Colleen touched a hand to her husband's arm. "We couldn't disappoint our girl, now could we?"

Patrick gave her a sheepish smile. "If you think we should."

"I do." As Patrick evaluated his own clothing against Marvin's suit, she added, "But, there's no need for you to dress up any further, if that's what concerns you."

A small sigh of relief passed from Patrick. "Well,

then—"

"Marvin, are you over here?" Jenna called out from the front door.

"He is. He's decided to have tea with us, while he waited for you to get home. You're welcome to join us." Though he'd died many years before, Patrick hadn't lost the manners his wife insisted upon and he stood as Jenna entered the room. "That is if you have the time."

"I'm sorry, I'm running so late, I better not." Jenna brushed a hand through her hair and smoothed her rumpled blouse. "I do appreciate the offer, though. And thanks for looking after this big lug for me. Marvin, could you come home, I need to talk to you about something."

"Sure thing, Jen. Just let me fini—"

"Now, please," Jenna insisted. A slight crease knit her brow and she bit at her lower lip.

Marvin downed his tea and pushed up out of his chair. "Colleen, your tea was excellent. It does work wonders. Thank you."

"You're entirely welcome, dear; anytime," Colleen replied. When Marvin turned to carry his cup to the kitchen, she touched his jacket sleeve. "Oh, there's no need for that."

"I can drop it in the sink."

"That's thoughtful of you, really it is. But what else does an old woman have to do? Now, you run along and take care of our girl."

Marvin put the cup down on the table next to Colleen, gave a slight wave, and hurried after her. "Jen, hon…"

He found her at home, leaning against the kitchen

counter, downing a glass of wine. There was a tear in the hem of her right pant leg, smudges of dirt on her blouse. "What happened? Where did you go?"

Jenna threw herself into his arms. "Oh, Marv…"

Her quaking arms grasped at him. "What? What's wrong? Are you all right?" Though he knew it was impossible, being as she was dead and all, he pushed against her, to hold her out at arms' length, to make sure she hadn't been hurt. It was one habit of the living he didn't want to lose. Jenna tightened her grip. This was unlike the woman he'd met and fallen in love with. That woman had been strong and defiant, capable and ready for a fight at any turn. Though a bit of fear might be understandable since she'd only been dead a few days, she clung to him like a little girl. "What? Tell me."

She took a deep breath to gather her strength and pulled away. "I'm okay. Rattled, is all."

"Why? What happened?"

"Well, I heard a woman scream. I mean, not a scared kind of scream, Marv, this was a blood-curdling, frightened-for-her-life scream." Jenna knocked back the rest of her wine and poured another glass full. She held the bottle up in question and Marvin declined. "Then I heard the most foul-mouthed man yelling and threatening to kill her."

Marv's stomach dropped in dread. When Jenna was alive, she'd spent a lot of time working at a shelter for battered women, volunteering, doing what she could to help; she'd seen a lot of scarred bodies and souls. He feared where this was headed. "Is the woman okay? Did she get away?"

"Uh, yeah… But…"

Marvin waited.

"I kind of helped, you know. And this man—not the one who'd been attacking his wife, or girlfriend, or whatever she is to him—this was a deadhead." Jenna stopped and a slight shiver went through her. "Marvin, he looked at me, he scowled, and shook his head. He opened his mouth and I ran. I don't even know what he said, I ran so fast to get out of there."

Though Marvin knew perfectly well what her answer would be, he asked anyway. "What did he look like? Describe him."

"A big man. Not heavy-big, tall big. He had on dirty, ratty clothes. You know, tattered and threadbare, and a tam hat, like the kind you used to see men wearing on golf courses. The closest comparison I could make right now is he reminded me a bit of the character Will Smith played in *Bagger Vance*."

Marvin chuckled. "You're starting to sound like Tommy. Everything gets equated to a movie."

Jenna ignored his interjection. "But it wasn't that that scared me. Maybe it was my imagination, but I swear he started to get bigger."

Because Jenna stood there in the kitchen with him, based on his own experience Marvin knew the answer to his next question, too. "The man who accosted the woman, the live guy, what happened to him?"

"Oh, he'll be fine." Jenna waved a dismissive hand. "He just fell and bumped his head. Marvin—"

Marvin's voice became stern. "But you had something to do with his fall, didn't you?"

"Well, yeah. Marvin, I couldn't let him keep at her. I couldn't! She was bloody and bruised and he was pointing a gun at her and—"

Marvin pushed to the point. "What were you going to do before you heard the deadhead's voice?"

"Well, I managed to knock the gun out of that asshole's hand and it skittered across the sidewalk. Naturally, I ran and picked it up. Not that I could do it, I yelled at the man to stop or I'd shoot, but he kept beating her, Marv. So, I yelled again and that's when I heard a real deep, loud voice—like it came from the depths of the earth, you know—say my name. I turned, saw him and…" Her body quivered again. "I dropped the gun and ran."

Marvin grabbed her upper arms with both hands. "Don't ever try something like that again. Do you hear me? Ever!" Then he pulled her into a bear hug and held her until she stopped shaking. "Okay now? Better?"

Jenna nodded her head against his chest. "What happened, Marv? Who was that…man? How did he know my name?"

"I don't know. I suspect they know who we *all* are." A violent shudder ran down his spine.

Jenna raised her face to look at him. "What was that about?"

"You're lucky. You got off with a warning."

"What do you mean?"

"I told you about Jason and what he did to me, remember?"

Jenna shook her head. "I remember that name, but all you said was, 'You don't even want to know.'"

"Well, then, in that case, I was right the first time. You don't want to know." Marvin looked at the clock. "You better get ready, or you'll be late for your own funeral."

Jenna pulled away from him, noticed the serious

expression on his face, and laughed. "Don't be ridiculous." She strode to the bedroom to clean up and change.

Chapter 4

As Tommy predicted, Davy stood in the lobby of the Davis Funeral Home near the doors to the chapel; the same room Jenna had booked for Marvin's visitation. When Jenna walked through the lobby, an arm linked through one of Marvin's, and Tommy and Mike following them, Davy smiled with appreciation.

He threw his arms open for a hug. "Oh, my, don't you look scrumptious. I knew it, I knew that would be the perfect dress."

Jenna laughed, accepted the air kisses, and then twirled around for him. The full-skirted, shimmering Kelly Green chiffon highlighted her green eyes and set off her auburn hair. The gown splayed out from her body and exposed the silver heels he'd chosen for her. The diamond earrings and matching choker-style necklace borrowed for the occasion glittered. "You like it?"

"Oh, honey, you are going to turn heads for sure." Davy shot a quick aside to Marvin, "Diane's not the prettiest diva in town anymore. She'll positively look like a frump now!"

Before Davy could throw open the doors, Tommy interrupted him, and in his excitement rushed right through Marvin. "Dude! Wait. I want to do the intro this time."

"Jesus H., hippie! Don't do that." Marvin slapped

through the back of Tommy's head. Marv would never get used to the buzz it caused when some deadhead brushed through him in a rush like that. For him, it was almost as bad as a living person knocking into him; not quite, but almost.

"Sorry, Marvin."

"And who would this Diane person be?" Jenna poked a finger through Marvin's shoulder.

"Oh, this woman at Marvin's funeral—" Davy stopped when he noticed the scowl on Marvin's face. "Oh, you know, just someone who thought she'd hit the jackpot when she laid eyes on Marvin here. Of course, she changed her mind quite quickly when he made a beeline to your side. If she shows up today to judge the new competition, she'll be positively green with envy."

Tommy flung the big double mahogany doors wide and stepped into the room with a flourish. "Ladies and gentlemen, I introduce to you Ms. Jenna Wilson!"

"Nice save," Marvin whispered to Davy.

When Jenna stepped forward through the archway as Davy had instructed, a round of applause and murmurs spread through the discarnate crowd. She smiled and waved. At the nods of approval from the ladies, and the discernible words of "gorgeous" and "hot" from the men, she broke into a lilting laugh. More than one man moved in to greet her and stopped short when Marvin stepped to Jenna's side, and she hooked her arm through his. The number and din of deadheads muted the small crowd of living mourners who sat in the first few rows.

It was apparent Mr. Davis, the proprietor of the Davis Funeral Home, had done some remodeling since Marvin's wake when the place still had outdated folding chairs. The wallpaper had been replaced by a dove gray paint, a white chair rail splitting the wall ran the entire perimeter. Thick, charcoal-colored carpeting covered the floor, save for the center aisle to ease movement of sometimes extraordinarily heavy, unwieldy coffins.

The layout of things hadn't changed, though. With a spray of roses adorning the top, Jenna's casket took center stage in the small alcove at the front of the room on its wheeled dais. Ceiling can-lights shone against the burnished metal, augmented by candelabras at either end. Several small funeral arrangements, sent by the law firm, had been placed to the left side of the alcove, and an easel held a display of photos on the right, though the flowers to shield the base of it had been supplied by Mr. Davis (included in the bill, of course).

Jenna and Marvin both let go sounds of surprise as they made their way to the front.

"Oh, my God, Marv." Jenna nudged Marvin and pointed to his family, seated in the front row of the new, padded-seat pews, on the left; the 'family side' as she recalled her one-time future mother-in-law had referred to it. "What are they doing here?"

"Who?"

"Your mother and father."

Sure enough, as Marvin followed her pointing finger, there sat Madelyn sobbing into her husband Morton's shoulder as if her world had tumbled down around her ears.

"I expected to see your brother, but why would your parents come? And what's with the crocodile tears? Your mother hated me."

"Jen, for the hundredth time, my mother did not

hate you."

"Bullshit, Marvin. I got nothing but cold, icy stares from that woman from the day you brought me to meet them."

Marvin heaved a sigh. While Jenna may have been born Jewish, it was certainly obvious none of the foster homes she'd grown up in were Jewish families; she would never get a handle on how things worked. From his mother's perspective, his brother, David, was the logical choice for Jenna after Marvin's death. "She's here and sobbing because now David won't be able to marry you."

Jenna ignored the statement. Though David had kept in touch after Marv's death, they knew there would be no chance of a relationship. Jenna considered David to be too much of a pleaser, too much of a mama's boy for her taste, and he'd been well aware of the fact. "Speaking of your brother, where is he?"

Mike spoke up from behind them. "Over there in the corner, talking to Mr. Davis."

Jenna scowled at the old funeral director who'd pushed her financial envelope to the limit when she'd made the arrangements for Marvin. "I don't know what he's charged JoAnne for this, but thank goodness your father stepped in and made him lower the bill on yours," she told Marvin.

"He also paid it for you."

"I know that, Marv. You could give a person a chance to finish before you butt in."

Marv spread his hands out in question. "What? I was just sayin'."

"Well, so was I." Jenna slapped at his arm and her hand breezed through it. They looked to the right side of the room to find her boss, JoAnne, tears streaming down her face, seated with a moderate contingent from the law firm Jenna worked for, where she'd been promoted to full-fledged paralegal a few weeks before she tumbled down the stairs of the condo building in a tangle of limbs with Mrs. McClaskey.

Larry, the young lawyer Jenna dated for a very brief period after Marvin's death, sat at the far end and dabbed his eyes with a handkerchief. Marvin pointed to him. "Get a load of that schmuck, will ya? From the looks of him, you'd think he really cared."

"Well, maybe he did, Marv. How do you know what he feels right now?"

"Maybe I know plenty." Marvin nudged her. "Hey, who left you alone at the hospital after the golf course accident?"

"I wasn't alone, Jo was with me." Jenna pulled away a little to turn and look at him. "Besides, who was it that smacked me with the golf ball in the first place?"

Marvin tried to cover his guilt with a sheepish grin. "What can I say? I missed you." He shrugged. "So sue me."

"I'll sue you all right. How about if I deck you one?" Jenna pointed to JoAnne. "Oh, God, look at her, Marv… That breaks my heart… I don't suppose there's anything I can do to let her know I'm okay, is there?"

"Well, you could—" Marvin started.

"No." Tommy caught Jenna's arm. "Not allowed."

Jenna pulled away and moved in JoAnne's direction.

"Oh, come on, Tommy. That's not entirely true. She could leave her some signals," Marvin argued.

"I wouldn't go breaking any rules right now."

Tommy looked around the room and then leaned into him in a conspiratorial way. "Jason and Nancy are probably keeping real close watch right now. Dude, I'd keep a very low profile for a while if I was you. Or do you want one of them to come for you again?"

Marvin shuddered thinking about the images he'd been shown, what his existence would've been like if he had succeeded in killing Jenna. Though Nancy would replace the old black man as The Keeper in their region and seemed a bit gentler, he didn't want either one of them coming for him again. "No. But I'm just talking about—"

Tommy's face lit up in a grin. "Besides, you two are going to be way too busy planning the wedding."

Davy rushed over, bumping through the crowd without regard for the buzzing sensation it caused to anyone. "Wedding? Did I hear wedding?"

"Yeah! Isn't it great?" Tommy beamed.

"Who's getting married? Why haven't I heard about this?"

Tommy pointed to Marvin, and then to Jenna, who had already moved to hover over JoAnne. Jenna reached out to place her hands on the distraught woman's shoulders and leaned in to hug her. "Jo, I'm so sorry. I don't know what to say to make you understand."

JoAnne brushed at the fly that buzzed past her ear, hugged herself, and bitched through her sniffles to no one in particular. "Jesus Christ, it's the middle of fucking winter, and they have the air conditioning on? The chill runs right through to the bones."

Davy, sporting a big smile, started waving his hands in excitement. "Oh, my God. Oh my God. This is fabulous!" He latched onto Tommy's arm. "When? Where? Who's doing her dress? Oh my God, I can't wait. No, stop right there. This is impossible."

"Why? Aren't deadheads allowed to marry?" Mike piped in.

Davy let go of Tommy to address Mike's question. "No, no, no. That's not what I mean. Of course, it's never been done before—Well, that I know of, and believe me I'd know if it had. No, I'm going to do this for them. It'll be the biggest wedding the world has ever seen. It'll put Di's wedding to shame." Davy turned to Tommy again with an air of professionalism, gazing past his shoulder. "Okay, when do we start? I'm seeing St. Patrick's Cathedral."

"Uh, Davy, you do know they're Jewish, right?" Mike nudged him with an elbow.

Davy waved him off. "Okay, so the ballroom at the Plaza. No, wait. That'll be too small."

Mike interrupted his train of thought again. "Um…How do you propose to do a wedding in New York when we're all here in Dayton?"

"Oh my God, I have to go. I have to think about this. Tell her I'll be in touch." Davy threw a wave over his shoulder and left in such a rush he didn't see or acknowledge Diane standing at the back of the room staring at Jenna in jealous awe.

Chasing after him, Diane called, "Davy! Wait!"

Unaware of the commotion among the dead over the impending nuptials of her oldest son, Madelyn sauntered to the display board where pictures had been placed into a collage. With a loud, braying moan that sounded like a wounded walrus, she brought all chatter to dead silence.

David rushed to her side and admonished her in gruff but hushed tones, "Ma, stop. You're making a spectacle."

Madelyn sobbed into her son's chest, but still managed to be heard at the back of the visitation room. "Again? Again I'm shoved out? Again I get *gornisht*—nothing."

Marvin stomped over to stand behind his mother. "And when did you ever agree to be in a picture with Jen? Never, that's when. Not even when we got engaged."

"You see how they treat me, David? The woman's own mother-in-law?"

"Ma, what are you talking about? She and Marvin weren't married, you know that."

Madelyn raised her head and sniffed. "Well, they would've been—if she hadn't killed him." She issued another loud bray. "Oh, my poor baby."

"Jenna did not kill me. But, if you aren't careful," Marvin warned, and shook a fist at her. "I'm gonna help her kill *you* when she gets fed up with your nonsense."

David grabbed his mother by the elbow and, shaking his head, squired her toward her seat. "And you wonder why there are no pictures of you."

"Oh, Morton." Sorrow laced Madelyn's voice. "Does a mother's pain never end?"

"It could end pretty rapidly if you keep it up," Marvin threatened from across the room.

"Dude… Give it rest." Tommy grabbed Marvin by the arm to lead him back to Jenna, who was well used to Marvin's outbursts and had continued to think of ways to console JoAnne and ignored the entire ordeal.

Morton grabbed Madelyn's sleeve and pulled her

down next to him. "Madelyn, if you don't stop, I'm leaving. You can walk back to Westchester."

"Yeah, Marv, don't start with that stuff again. It makes the rest of us nervous as hell," Mike interjected with a wave of his hand at the crowd of deadheads who had moved to give Marvin a wide berth.

"Okay, okay." Marvin sighed.

Everyone settled down and returned to hushed tones until it was time to leave for the cemetery. The morose background music faded, overhead lighting in the room intensified dimming the effects of the twin candelabras on either end of the casket. The brightened lights caused a beam to reflect off the coffin and shine directly in JoAnne's direction. She shielded her eyes and cursed under her breath. "Dammit! Jenna, you knew how I hated this shit, why did you have to dump it on me?"

Mr. Davis signaled to David and Morton who moved toward the casket and stood waiting for the other pall bearers to join them. JoAnne had asked the managing partner of the law firm and Larry to do the honors. The partner made his way from the back of the room. Larry, however, was nowhere in sight.

"Hold on a minute." JoAnne stood. The heels of her shoes pounded against the tile floor and echoed through the room, making her anger evident.

It had all the makings of a confrontation Marvin couldn't resist watching. "This I gotta see." He pulled free from Jenna and followed JoAnne.

When she didn't spot Larry in the small lobby, she walked toward the front door. "Probably in your usual spot, like you do at the office? Outside smoking instead of working?" She pushed the heavy door open and held it with one hand as she scanned the sidewalk in front of the building. Popping back in, she called out, her voice echoing through the tiled space, "Larry! Larry! Where the hell are you?"

He emerged from the men's room, a cloud of cigarette smoke trailing after. "Sorry, I didn't think I had to ask permission to take a leak."

"Don't get smart with me, you asshole."

Once Larry had ambled past her, he mumbled. "Screw you."

JoAnne lunged after him, grabbing his jacket sleeve. "What was that?"

"Nothing."

"That's what I thought. Now get your ass in there and do your job."

Larry whirled on her, his face red with rising anger. "Don't pull this crap on me. Not here."

"Yeah? Or what?"

"You know, you may think—" He nipped the remark and strode away.

JoAnne smiled. "I'm pleased the argument the other day, when I told you you'd be a pall bearer, hit its mark"

Jenna laughed in delighted glee when she regaled Marvin with the details of it in all their glory. JoAnne strutted to where Larry had been perched on a landscape planter and poked a finger into his bicep when he insisted she couldn't boss him around. "You think not? Might I remind you *again* who actually runs the firm? I know everything that goes on in this place and the partners keep me here for a reason. And that's to keep slackers like you in line. Now, you'll be at Jenna's funeral, you'll carry her body with dignity, not because she was a co-worker, you asshole, but because you can at least show her the respect you didn't give her when you were trying to get in her pants."

"I never—"

She pointed a finger at him. "Don't even go there. I know everything. Including the fact you never even bothered to call and ask how she was after the incident at the golf course last spring."

Larry got off the landscape planter that stood at the edge of the employee parking lot, where he'd been sitting, and puffed out his chest. "And if I refuse?"

"Then, watch out motherfucker. Because I'll make sure you draw every piece-of-shit case that walks in the door. If it wasn't for me, you'd be a single-shingle in a run-down, grimy office somewhere, handling quickie divorces."

"I'm better than that!"

A grim smile spread on JoAnne's lips. "Yes, you are. But only because I make it happen."

Her heels again echoing against the tile of the funeral home lobby, JoAnne followed Larry back into the visitation room, with Marvin close on hers, where Larry took his place at the foot end of Jenna's coffin.

Marvin stepped to Jenna's side, wrapped her arm around his, and they moved to take the lead in the procession. "You know, It's a good thing I met you first, otherwise I'd have gone after her in a flash. I love a woman who stands up to schmucks like him."

The slightest chuckle escaped Jenna.

"What's funny about that?"

"You couldn't handle her. Besides, she's a little old for you, Marvin."

Chapter 5

The drive to the cemetery, where Mr. Davis had managed to secure the burial plot for Jenna right next to Marvin's, was uneventful; for the breathing mourners, anyway. Though JoAnne liked Marvin's father and brother, she'd had about all she could stand of Madelyn. She made Mr. Davis provide a second car for them with "damn the expense!" and sat alone in the back of the lead limousine. Or so she thought.

Marvin, Jenna, and Mike occupied the seat opposite her. Tommy, as usual, sat up front next to the driver and, laughing, played with every power button he could find on the dashboard. Heat blasted through the vent system and switched without notice to ice cold a/c; the radio changed stations up and down the dial; the passenger seat rose and fell, moved forward and back, reclined and returned upright. It all left the driver muttering aloud about how he would explain to his boss that "a brand new, seventy-thousand-dollar vehicle had some major electrical problems." The poor man groaned, "Hope to God I can get through the job without needing a flippin' tow truck."

Even though the sun blared down on the group of mourners, it was a calm, cold day. Not a wisp of wind added to the chill factor. David still made short but sweet work of a eulogy. When Mr. Davis held out the ceremonial shovel, David took it, and walked to

JoAnne. "Here, we'll do this together."

Jenna stepped to the mound of dirt that would fill in her grave. She grabbed a handful and tossed it in before a startled "NO" burst from the crowd of deadheads who'd gathered.

A gasp rose from the living. Some gaped around in fright and backed away. Madelyn let loose with a piercing shriek, clutched her husband's arm with both hands in a death grip. "Holy Mother of Mary! Morton, what the hell was that?"

"Ow!" Morton yanked his arm free. "It had to be a gust of wind."

"What? What did I do?" Jenna gaped around the crowd of deadheads for an answer. Though Madelyn's outburst sure explained where Marvin had gotten his favorite turn of phrase when something took him by surprise.

"You just scared the crap out of everyone. You have to time it, Jen," Marv admonished, and laughed along with the rest of the dead, who now found his mother's reaction quite humorous. "You wait for them to toss a shovelful and throw yours at the same time."

Mike waved him off. "Oh, Brody, give her a break. She's still new around here. She'll catch on."

"Yeah, besides, Marvin," Tommy offered, "maybe it woke some people up."

"Are you saying my brother delivered a boring eulogy? Is that what you're saying, hippie?" Marvin laughed and scruffed the hair on the top of Tommy's head.

"Dude, the coif!" Tommy pulled away in mock horror, as he always did whenever Marvin messed the long mane of hair that looked as if it hadn't seen a comb since 1969.

The bulk of the deadheads in attendance drifted off, still laughing, leaving the core friends to the finality of a life. The small group of living lined up to honor their friend by tossing a small shovel of dirt over the lowered coffin, murmured a final goodbye, and headed back to their lives. All except Madelyn, who stood stock still in the spot she'd run to, twenty feet away, after Morton had yanked himself free.

David called out to her. "Ma? Come on, Ma. You're the last one."

Madelyn shook her head.

"Ma! Come on. What are you afraid of?"

"Gust of wind, my *tuches*," Madelyn replied, looking around the cemetery, her eyes darting from plot to plot, as if she'd spy a ghoulish-looking Jenna rising out of the ground like Fruma Sarah from *Fiddler on the Roof*, with hands like claws ready to attack. "That was no gust of wind. It was her."

Morton rolled his eyes skyward. "Don't be a *shmendrik*. You want these people, her friends, her co-workers, to think you're a dummy?"

"She hates me. I can feel it."

"She didn't hate you, Ma."

Jenna turned her head away from Marvin, in the hope that he wouldn't hear her. "I'm sure the feeling was mutual."

Marvin poked her arm. "I heard that."

Still, Madelyn wouldn't budge. "She never liked me. David, you know this. Help your mother. You... You do it for me."

"She thought *you* didn't like *her*, that's why she stayed so distant." David crossed the expanse of grass and tugged on his mother's arm. "Now, come on."

"No, David. No, I'm afraid. What if she reaches up to take me with her? I'd die of a heart attack right there."

"You're not making sense, Ma." David paused for a long sigh. "You know, maybe if you show her this last respect, maybe she'll decide to like you."

She looked up at her son. "You think, maybe?"

"Jesus Christ, Madelyn. What the fuck." JoAnne, tired of the woman's shenanigans, tromped over to the mound of dirt, grabbed a handful and stalked over to her. "It's freezing cold. Now, here." She grabbed Madelyn's hand and shoved the dirt into it. "I don't care if you throw it from here, just do it."

Madelyn straightened her shoulders and glared at JoAnne, then uttered a "Hmph." She looked down at the dirt in her hand, tossed her head, and walked to the edge of the open grave with purposeful strides. With David standing behind her, she looked down and slowly released the dirt. "I'm sorry, honey. I really am."

"Was that so hard?" JoAnne clapped her hands together above the yawning grave to remove any traces of dirt. "Now, can we get the hell out of here?"

David placed a hand on his mother's shoulder. "See, she didn't reach out from the grave to hurt you."

A wistful smile came to Madelyn's lips, and she shook her head and sighed. "She was a good person, wasn't she, David? A nice woman."

David rolled his eyes. "Yes, she was, Ma."

Madelyn looked up at her youngest son. "So, see? You should've listened to your mother."

"What do you mean?"

Madelyn linked her arm around David's and the

two started walking back to the waiting limousine. "You should've married. I told you to marry her, didn't I? Maybe if you'd listened to your mother, maybe the poor thing would still be here with us, instead of lying in the cold ground."

Marvin broke into a hearty, full belly-laugh. "That woman will never change"

Chapter 6

The laugh cut short when Marvin saw Nancy leaning against one of the sleek black limousines. He greeted her with a nervous smile. "I was wondering if you would show up here, since I didn't see you at the funeral home. How've you been?"

"I'm good, Marvin, I'm good." Nancy turned her attention to Jenna. "Are you going to introduce us, or are you going to stand there staring out into space?"

Marvin didn't quite catch her response. His attention had been drawn to a large maple tree in the distance, its leaves had long since exposed dead-looking branches like a tangle of twisted limbs. A man stood watching and, Marvin knew, listening and hearing every word. Even from far away a brightness, intelligence, and intensity burned in the man's eyes that had always been hard for Marvin to miss.

After a half-hearted wave in greeting to Jason, Marvin shook his head. "Where are my manners? Colleen would be scowling at me right now. This is my fiancée, Jenna. Jenna, Nancy. Remember I told you about meeting her on my birthday cruise?"

"I don't believe you did, Marvin." Jenna accepted Nancy's extended hand though she gave the woman a thorough inspection, and checked Marvin's body language. As if satisfied nothing had gone on between them, she added, "In any case, it's a pleasure."

"Likewise." Nancy smiled and nodded her chin toward Jenna's gravesite. "Can I talk to you for a minute?"

A brief questioning expression crossed Jenna's face. "Sure, I guess."

Marvin went pale, if that was possible, and shot a quick, nervous glance toward Jason. "Uh, is there something wrong?"

Nancy ignored his question and led Jenna across the dormant grass, leaving Jason to deal with Marvin.

Jason's lips never moved, yet Marvin got his answer, loud and clear. "Don't you worry 'bout it none, Marvin. I think everythin' gon' be all right. Leastwise, I hope."

"Hey," Marvin called out to Nancy when he heard engines turn over. "We're going to miss our ride." He hooked a thumb over his shoulder to indicate the two limos that began rolling away.

"No problem, dude." Tommy jumped onto the hood of the lead car and pushed his hand through the metal.

The car stalled and an apparently aggravated JoAnne banged on the window that separated her from the frustrated driver, who squirmed in his seat.

"Not a good idea, Tommy," Mike told him. "Let them go, we can catch a bus."

"Okay." Tommy shrugged, twisted his arm around a bit. The engine fired up on a second attempt, the cars drove off along the narrow road, and Tommy and Mike went to stand with Marvin.

"What do you figure this is about?" Mike pointed in the direction of Jenna and Nancy.

Marv jutted his chin at the women. "She tried to

help someone this morning but, from what I could gather, it looked more like she was trying to shoot some guy."

"Dude… Not good."

Once they were out of Marvin's hearing range, Nancy stopped, took Jenna by the upper arms and turned Jenna to face her. "There was an incident…between you and the living."

Jenna's mood turned dark at the memory of the beating. Recalling the awful visage that called out her name, fright stabbed her in the stomach. Stammering, she backed away from Nancy.

"I understand what you were trying to do. But, it's best if you know right now, there are rules here. We are not allowed to mess with the living world." Nancy stopped her narrative for a moment and changed tactics in an effort to ease Jenna's fright. "Don't get me wrong, all of us pull pranks from time to time; harmless stuff. It's fun to watch people's confusion when we've hidden something from them and put it back, or see them shudder if they've walked through one of us. Now, I apologize if this comes across as some kind of lecture, but…"

The change in tactic, and the softness of voice, calmed Jenna until Nancy directed her gaze to Jason, who waited. Jenna let loose with a quick, frightened yelp. "That's the—Why did he come after me?"

Nancy reached out to lay a calming hand on Jenna's arm. "He wasn't coming after you, he wanted to stop you."

"Why? I was just trying to help that girl. What was happening to her, well it just—it's not right!"

"He knows that. But you interfered in his work."

Jenna's indignant, stubborn streak bubbled to the surface. "How can trying to save someone be wrong? That doesn't make sense."

****

From where he stood, Marvin couldn't hear what was being said, but he was very familiar with the expression on Jenna's face—the stance she adopted. He wanted to step in, to call out, *Oh, please, kiddo, don't. Don't argue, don't cop an attitude. It could get you killed. Well, sort of.* He took a step in their direction and stopped dead in his tracks when he heard Jason's warning.

"Uh-uh. You jes' stay right where you is, son. Don't you go getting' in the middle of dis. Ain't none of yo affair."

Marvin turned toward the frail looking old man. It was all for show; the clothes, the unkempt, homeless look, the dialect. All meant to blend in with the multitudes of the dead. Few deadheads took the opportunity to give Jason more than a passing glance, but Marvin knew better. He'd seen the intelligence in those dark eyes the first time he'd run across him on the street in front of the condo building. He'd experienced the change that could happen in a moment. "But, I want to help."

"I know you do. But, dis our job, keepin' you folks in line. Now, you listen to me, Marvin. You jes stay where you is."

Hearing nothing but Marvin's answers, Tommy asked, "Dude, what's he saying?"

"Nothing." A heaviness burned in Marvin's lungs, like he dove too deep into an ocean. His shoulders slumped. He turned around again and watched the love of his life take a risk he knew from personal experience could swallow her whole. Tommy and Mike threw protective arms across his shoulders and he gave each one a wan smile.

Nancy stood silent for a moment, searching for an answer that would return a sense of calm. Her response was even and deliberate. "Jenna, she would've been okay, the man would've died. You changed that."

"I don't understand. How?"

Nancy upped her game. "What is so difficult to understand? You took the gun."

"I sure as hell didn't see anyone else moving in to help!"

"Because it isn't for us to do."

"Well, if you don't help people why was *he* there?" Jenna pointed an accusing finger at Jason.

"To remove that abuser from any plane of existence, except into one of his own suffering. It's what he does." Nancy corrected herself, "What *we* do. It's how we police our world. You'll just have to accept what I'm saying, because believe me, as Marvin could tell you—if he had the strength to relive it—you don't want to experience it. You don't want to see it."

"I'm sorry, I can't stand by and watch someone get beat up."

Nancy shook her head. "Well, find a better way to help than trying to kill someone."

"Like?" Jenna challenged.

"I don't know. I'm just giving you fair warning. If you keep it up, Jason will have no choice."

Nancy didn't do much to veil the threat of consequences and Jenna softened. "What do you mean?"

Taking Jenna's hands in hers, Nancy said, "It means, what you saw of him this morning was nothing more than a shadow of the hell he could put you in. Please, for your sake; for Marvin's. Find a better way." She let go of Jenna's hands and walked away.

Jenna turned to watch the small backhoe push the mound of dirt into her burial site. Her lips trembled in anger as much as in fear. A sensation of pain surprised her when she bit down on her lower lip in thought. She touched a fingertip to it, then opened her purse, retrieved a small compact and adjusted it to see how badly she'd hurt herself. There was no gash, not even a tiny droplet of blood. "Huh. Well, that's interesting."

Marvin, Tommy, and Mike stood silent, waiting for Jenna, as Nancy strode away.

Without looking anyone directly in the eye, Jenna marched past them with a gruff, "Come on, let's go."

Tommy rushed over and matched her stride. "You want to talk about it?"

"What's to talk about? If Nancy thinks she, or anyone else for that matter, can stop me from protecting someone who's being beat up, or threatened with a gun, when there's clearly something I can do to help, well…"

Mike and Marvin followed, but stayed a few paces behind to give Tommy space and time to work his magic.

"Oh, of course you can help them. Just not by killing anyone, you know?"

"No, Tommy, I don't know! It's bullshit. Who put her in charge, anyway? Or this Jason guy? Why are any of us here if we can't do anything to help?" Her venting now over, Jenna turned morose. As silly as he could be

40

at times, unlike some folks who were as dead in the soul as they were in body when they arrived, Jenna knew Tommy felt it was his duty to help people transition. His connection with Marvin made it seem all that more important. Her voice faltered from anger to sadness, and her shoulders dropped in defeat. "It's just not fair."

Tommy grabbed hold of her arm and gave her his most charming impish expression and lop-sided smile. "Come here, let your Uncle Tommy give you a hug." Jenna hesitated and then allowed herself to be drawn into an embrace and began to sob. "It's okay, Jenna. Really. You'll get used to it." He took a peek to see that Mike and Marv had halted and were out of earshot and whispered, "I'll show you how to maneuver around here."

Jenna pulled out of the hug and gave him a questioning look. She kept her volume low and leaned next to his ear. "Are you saying what I think you are?"

Tommy shrugged with a sly smile. "Maybe. Now, come on, give your Uncle Tommy a smile?"

Jenna sniffled. "Oh, all right, you win." She linked an arm through Tommy's and held out the other for Marvin. "Let's go."

Marvin hooked her arm through his, and Tommy offered his other to Mike. "Dudes, I'm suddenly starved. What say we go haunt a nice classy restaurant and have some fun?"

Chapter 7

Several weeks after her funeral, Jenna sat next to Marvin on the balcony of their condominium, both with steaming cups of coffee, and enjoyed the sounds of the wakening city. Tires whined as traffic increased in dribs and drabs. The echoes of clomping footsteps crawled up the front of the building as people (living and dead) began appearing on the sidewalks below in growing numbers.

Marvin shuddered when a bus rolled past the building. "It still gives me the creeps."

"What does?"

"I swear I can still see blood on the pavement down there," Marvin said, pointing to the spot in the road where he'd lain after he stepped in front of the bus.

"Oh, stop with the drama already." Jenna nudged him with a shoulder.

"Well, excuse me for—" The sight of a moving van pulling to the curb in front of their building cut Marvin's remark short. "Huh, wonder what that's about."

"Colleen and Patrick told me the family behind us is moving out."

"Really?"

"Yeah, there was something about the board forcing them to sell."

"Good. Good riddance. The schmucks."

"Can they do that? The board, I mean."

"Well, if I hadn't noticed the hidden toy in his pocket it wouldn't have made it into the police report, and they probably would've gotten away with it."

Marvin remembered the morning Jenna and Mrs. McClaskey were found dead in a heap of tangled limbs at the bottom of the stairs. He had gone back down to the lobby to watch their bodies being loaded onto gurneys and wheeled out the front doors of the building.

He castigated the guys from the coroner's office who plopped them onto the stretchers with as much ceremony as the EMT's had used with him, which was to say none. "Hey, hey, hey, ya *schmucks*! Show a little respect, would ya?"

They went on about their business in complete silence, slammed the back doors of the wagons closed, and with short, curt waves to the cop still interviewing a resident, drove off.

Marvin glanced around the scene but didn't see the toy truck that caused Colleen to trip and lose her balance. "Huh, that's odd. Where's the stupid truck?" He looked in the hallway leading to the first floor units, poked into every corner, nook, and cranny of the lobby. Ready to give up, he noticed an odd bulge in the coat pocket of the man from his floor—the father who allowed his kids to play in the halls and on the stairs no matter how many times Marvin complained about it. A light touch to the shape told Marvin all he needed to know. "You son-of-a-bitch." He would've called him by name but, for the life of him, Marv couldn't remember it. "If you think you're gonna hide that and get away with your little rugrats killing that sweet old woman, not to mention my fiancée, you better think again."

Marv pushed fingers against the truck until they penetrated the fabric, wrapped them around the bed of the toy and, with as much finesse as he could muster, pulled it out. He turned it over in his hand and smiled. Retrieving it had been as easy as pulling the gun from the store display the time he'd tried to kill Jenna and shot himself in the head instead.

The neighbor, a confused expression on his face, looked down, altered his stance, and stuck a hand in his pocket. "What the—Where—"

The policeman glanced up from his notebook. "Did you lose something?"

"Oh, um…. No." The guy rattled keys in a pants pocket. "Just forgot which pocket I'd put my keys in."

"You lying sack of shit. You were looking for this." Marv tossed the truck. It dropped out of the air and landed upside down next to the newel post at the bottom step, its wheels spinning, just as Marvin had seen it the night before.

His neighbor tried and failed to hold in an audible gasp. The cop cast a quick glance at the truck, looked directly at the distraught resident, and shook his head. He bent over, grabbed the truck and confronted the man. "Drop something?"

The man let loose a nervous laugh. "Oh, um, yeah. I guess I did, huh?"

"Look, Mr. Sullivan, if this was the cause of the fall—and it was, wasn't it?" The policeman stared and waited until the man dropped his gaze in guilt. "It was obviously an accident. You didn't need to bullshit me. But, you shouldn't have tampered with the scene. I could get you on that, you know."

Marvin smacked himself in the forehead. "Sullivan, right." He hated to admit it, but Tommy had been correct. Though his brain cells worked here in the afterlife, they hadn't popped with new intelligence; he'd gotten no better with names. Of course, when he was alive he'd never put much effort into knowing his neighbors.

"Now," Officer Gentner continued, "I'll let you off on the charge of interfering with an investigation, but I'm gonna have to put into my report that your kid's toy was the cause of the fall, which killed the two victims."

"Oh, come on." Marvin leaned around the cop's shoulder to read the name tag and, though he knew the men wouldn't hear a single word (being as he was dead and all), he continued his rant. "Let me tell you something here, Officer Gentner, no matter how many times I warned this guy, he never cared. This is not the first time his brat's toys were left on the stairs. You go ask the Secretary of the association how many times I reported it. I told them. I told them one day someone's gonna get killed. Now look what's—"

Officer Gentner flipped to a second page to continue his report when Jenna's whispered voice rolled down from the top of the stairs. "Marvin... Marv!"

"Yeah?"

"You're yelling loud enough to wake the dead."

"Who's sleeping?"

Jenna appeared on the steps. "Did you once consider Colleen, or Patrick?"

"Sorry...I forgot. Guess I got too used to being the only dead guy around here."

"Well, just stop now. Come up and let them take

care of their business."

Marvin made it up five steps before he turned around and looked down at the two men. Glaring, he placed two fingers under his eyes, then pointed them at Sullivan. "I'm watching you, ya schmuck."

Marvin's reverie ended when Jenna nudged him. "I guess it was good that you caught Mr. Sullivan trying to cover it up. I mean, someone else in the building could've gotten hurt. You know, I still found toys in the hallway. Well, I just hope they're quiet." Jenna lifted her coffee cup to indicate the crew of movers, who'd jumped from the cab of the truck. "It's too early to be rattling and bumping dollies full of furniture and boxes down the stairs."

Marvin's entire response was, "Mmm."

"What should we do today?"

"I think Tommy wanted to go see some new movie."

"Which one?"

Marvin chuckled. "Who knows? He usually never makes up his mind until he gets there."

"Oh. Well, you know, I think I want to be out and about today. It's actually nice. No sense in wasting it sitting in a dark theater."

"You're coming to Epstein's with us, though, right?"

Jenna smiled at the distraught-but-expectant expression on his face. Marvin wanted to spend time together and knew she wanted to spend time with him, too. But all the same, she needed some space. As tough as it might be for him to admit, she'd begun to get used to handling life without him.

"What's the matter, Marvin? Does Tina scare you?

You need me to protect you?" she teased. "Of course, I'm going."

"What, you don't think she's scary? The woman runs around that place looking stricken with apoplexy." Marv played along, but his real concern was for Jenna's safety. He shuddered at the fate that awaited her if she pulled another stunt like she had the morning of her funeral and loathed to let her out of his sight. At least until she learned to stick to the rules, but he had his doubts that would happen any time soon.

Chapter 8

Despite Marvin's protest, Jenna left the boys sitting in the booth at Epstein's. She meandered down the street, turning her face to the warmth of the sun each time it peeked out from behind a bank of clouds. There was no rush to get anywhere, and she had no particular place in mind when she spotted a jewelry store across the street.

After watching the fun Tommy had playing in traffic just to see the reaction of drivers when they felt the cold chill run through them as their warm bodies collided with his dead one, she knew it couldn't hurt her. Still, she halted in the center of the street to avoid the oncoming vehicles.

Inside the store, she gazed at the sparkling gems and, once in a while, reached through the glass to pull one from the case. Unlike some dead folks, she took care that no one could see the merchandise flicker out of sight as she picked it up. To her knowledge she'd been alone in the jewelry store; well, if you didn't count the woman who stood haggling with the owner over the retail price of a charm bracelet for her granddaughter. A voice called her name and Jenna turned in surprise.

The woman wore a broad smile on her perfectly chiseled face. She brushed back a wave of thick, long blonde hair with one hand while extending the other in greeting. "I'm Diane. I'd been hoping to run into you sometime. I've heard so much about you."

Jenna accepted the hand and smiled. She wondered if this was the same Diane she'd heard Davy mention. If so, there was room for suspicion.

Diane barreled right along. "Isn't this just the best part of being dead? We can wander into any old store and take whatever we want and never have to worry about the bills. Oh, but would you look at this necklace." Without so much as a glance at the owner, Diane lifted it from its case and examined the large square-cut blue sapphire, surrounded by diamond baguettes on a heavy gold chain. She held it up to Jenna's throat. "This would look positively stunning on you."

"What would I wear it with? And for what?"

"For the wedding! Trust me, it's perfect."

"Uh, who told you there was going to be a wedding?"

"Why, Davy, of course." Diane laughed and tossed the necklace aside. It landed with a clatter on top of the glass case. The jeweler looked around, astonished. He hadn't heard the door chime, and the store was empty except for the bickering client. He gave the woman a quick, suspicious glare, thinking she had clearly picked it up and dropped it to put him off his game. He hurried over to put it back into its velvet box, and an expression of confusion painted his face when he found the glass doors still locked. Yet, he rushed back and leaned against his side of the display as if to prevent the woman from snatching anything further.

"Davy should forget it. It's a ridiculous idea."

"But, I think it's perfectly spectacular. He's a genius, you know. The gown he picked out for your funeral was stunning to say the least."

"He may be a genius, but a wedding isn't just out of the question, it's preposterous. I'm capable of taking care of myself. If I didn't need to be married while I was alive, I sure as hell don't need to be married now."

Diane looked up from the case of jewels she'd been studying. "Girl, you could be dangerous. But you know what? I think I *like* you."

"Gee, thanks." Jenna managed a smile at the backhanded compliment.

Diane peeked over at the jeweler, then snatched the necklace from the case and dumped it into her Gucci bag. Jenna huffed in disgust and went out the door. Outside the store, as she started to walk away, Diane slid an arm around Jenna's waist, and gave a small tug. "Hold on a minute, this could be fun."

The jeweler glanced over at the case and ran to stare down at the now-empty velvet perch with an expression of disbelief. Jenna and Diane couldn't hear the exchange of words because of the thick bullet-proof glass as he stormed his way back to confront her, but watched the customer dump the contents of her purse on the counter like a littered waterfall and turn out the pockets of her coat with such force one ripped clean off at the seams. The jeweler dropped down on all fours behind the counter. The woman made wild gestures as she intermittently stuffed her belongings back into her purse.

"That's awful! He's accusing that poor woman of stealing it."

Diane stared at Jenna, as if sizing up the situation, and muttered, "Oh, I'll put it back."

Diane walked through the window and dropped the

necklace onto the floor behind the counter. The man whirled around, snatched it into his hands, and stood; his face red in embarrassment. He approached his customer too late.

Spinning on her heels, the woman stomped to the door and pushed it open. "You can keep your crappy bracelet. It isn't worth ten percent of what you wanted, you *schiester*. And don't think I won't tell people what you accused me of."

Diane was still laughing when she exited the store. The woman stalked off down the sidewalk muttering and shaking her head. Jenna stared after her. "That was rather mean, don't you think?"

"No, not really. The guy does have an unbelievable mark-up." Diane grabbed Jenna's arm once again. "But come on, Miss Goody Two Shoes, there's a high-end boutique you're gonna love."

Quite a bit later, as the two wandered from store to store in the mall, Diane spotted Mike, Marvin, and Tommy cutting through the mall on the way back to the bus station to head for home. "Marvin! Look who I ran into. Honey, you never told me what an absolute delight your Jenna is."

"Diane…" Marv stuck out a hand in greeting. "You remember Mike and Tommy, don't you?" While Diane accepted Tommy's handshake without a word, Marvin leaned into Mike and whispered, "Oy. The last thing I need is two cats, who used up all nine lives, getting into a clawing competition."

Diane's eyes brightened and she held out her hand to Mike. "I don't believe I've had the pleasure."

Mike took her hand and smiled. "So, you're the infamous Diane that Davy has talked about."

She laughed and though she waved off the remark, still said, "Infamous, huh? I think I like the sound of that. But, Davy does go on about things, doesn't he?"

Tommy turned to Jenna. "We were just headed home to see if you might be hungry."

"Oh, how perfect!" Diane wrapped an arm through Mike's and pointed toward the mall exit. "I know just the place." She directed a knowing glance in Marvin's direction. "Have you ever gone to Mr. C's? It's an Italian place, but they make a really good steak. And the bar is always stocked with top-shelf."

Marvin's chin dropped to his chest and he sighed. With a swipe of his hand upside the back of Tommy's head he said, "Thanks a lot."

"Dude, don't blame me. I'm not the one who caused such a ruckus that the place got labeled as haunted."

"Haunted? What did you do, Marv?" Jenna hooked an arm through his and led the group through the mall toward the exit.

"Nothing. I don't know what he's talking about."

"Nothing? Dude, you landed a story in the newspaper." Tommy gave him a broad smile and a wink.

Marvin glared at him. "No one wants to hear about it, so just clam your trap."

Mike grabbed the back of Tommy's shirt. "Marvin here just got a little upset over a, uh, a steak dinner."

"Yeah," Tommy laughed. "It flew across the dining room and scared the bejesus out of everyone."

"Now, why would you do that, Marvin?" A second later Jenna stopped so short that her arm yanked through and free of Marvin's, and Diane and Mike lurched right through them. "Wait. I remember reading the story in the paper. It was during my date with Larry, wasn't it? It wasn't the waiter being clumsy and dumping the glass of water in Larry's crotch at all. It was you."

A sheepish smile spread over Marvin's face. "What can I say? I was just trying to cool him down a little bit, if you catch my drift."

"That's so sweet." Jenna smiled, hugged him, and kissed him on the cheek.

They linked arms and continued walking. Marvin let out a sigh of relief. He may have failed at dodging a real bullet, but at least he managed to duck a figurative one.

Chapter 9

After several weeks of running into Diane numerous times, and in a variety of places, Jenna caught on it was deliberate. She didn't exactly like the woman, but for some reason Jenna couldn't quite explain to Marvin when he asked, Diane seemed to be growing on her. Jenna promised they would spend the day browsing through stores and left Epstein's Deli earlier than usual, leaving the guys lounging over endless cups of coffee. The plan was to run home and change into something more acceptable to the high-browed, *Well, okay*, Jenna admitted her bias, *snooty woman*.

A small moving van stood at the curb in front of their condominium. The doors to the building were propped open and a man emerged, loaded down with boxes. Wondering who was moving out, she quickened her pace. Jenna got to the top of the stairs, saw the door to her and Marvin's place standing open, and let out a shriek. "What the hell is going on?"

She rushed through the entryway and followed the noise coming from their bedroom. Two men stood pulling clothes from the drawers and closet. They made no attempt to neatly fold anything. Blouses, skirts, and pants were rolled into balls, items were stripped from hangers, carelessly bundled, and tossed into open boxes.

Stunned, Jenna stood rigid until her anger boiled over. "What do you think you're doing? Stop! Those are my clothes. You can't take my stuff. What am I going to wear?" The men continued on with their task. Jenna stormed over to the box and began picking things up, draping them on hangers, and putting them back where they belonged. "Who told you that you could come in here and take my things?"

The guy cleaning out the closet froze in place. A dress he stuffed into the box at his feet was back in the closet, its hanger swaying as if a sudden breeze had cropped up. He turned to see if the window was opened and then believing he'd jostled items in his careless rush returned to the work at hand. He jumped and let out a frightened squeal when he found two more pieces once again in the closet. "Clancy. Clancy!"

"What's up?"

"Man, you tell me."

Clancy looked up from taping a box closed. "Is that all you managed to do so far, Ben? The closet is still full. You better put on some speed, man. We don't have all day and I'm not—"

"I'm not doing anything but making tracks outta here." Ben turned on his heels and ran out the door, pushing past Dan who was returning after dumping an armload of boxes into the van.

"Hey, knock me down, why don't you. Jesus..." Dan walked into the master bedroom to retrieve another load and found Clancy with his back against the far wall, as pale as a glass of pasteurized milk. "What the fuck is wrong with you two?"

Clancy pointed at the closet where a bright red skirt had popped into view, swinging. Dan followed the finger, shrugged, and yanked it out of the closet. "It's a real purdy thing, Clancy. You fancy puttin' it on, do ya?" He held it out for inspection. "I don't think it'll fit."

"You give that back!" Jenna tried to yank it out of his hands but, each time she tugged on it, her hand glided through the fabric and came up empty. "Let go, you dumb hick. That's a Dior for God's sake." Dan stood shaking the item in the air. "I said let go," Jenna growled, and punched him in the head.

Dan dropped the hanger with a howl and a sharp gasp, and grabbed at his temple. "Son-of-a-bitch." The pain shooting across his forehead reminded him of the intense ice-cream headaches he got as a kid at Cedar Point. Clutching his head, he dropped to his knees.

Clancy ran out of the building so fast he stumbled into Ben and the two of them ended up in a heap on the sidewalk alongside the panel van. They untangled themselves and stood up. Clancy retrieved the cigarette that had been knocked from his grasp and rolled into the gutter. He put it to his lips with a quaking hand, drew a large puff of smoke into his lungs, and held it as long as he could before letting it out in a slow, steady stream. The residual smoke mingled with the chilled air in wafts of steam when he talked, "Holy shit, man. What the hell was that up there?"

"I got no fuckin' idea, bro. It's like the place is haunted, or some shit."

They stood at a safe distance away, staring at the open lobby doors to the building, when Dan appeared. "What the hell are you two doing down here? Get back up there. We've got a lot of work to do."

"Are you crazy? I ain't going back in there."

Clancy dropped his cigarette, ground it out and immediately pulled another Camel from the crumpled pack. He offered one to Ben and they both chased the flame of the lighter Clancy grasped in trembling hands until the ends glowed scarlet and they choked on the overheated acrid smoke.

"Well, you either go back up and finish, or get canned and the court reconsiders your community service."

Ben and Clancy looked at each other, down at the sidewalk, up at Dan, and looked again at one another.

"What's it going to be, guys?"

The two men took long pulls on their cigarettes. "Well, I need this," Ben said. "I'd rather spend a few hours dealing with a haunted house than go to fuckin' jail." He flicked the butt of the cigarette into the street, where it got smashed by a passing car, and headed toward the building.

By the time Ben got to the waiting Dan, Clancy had bolstered his nerve and followed. With Dan at the rear, the three trudged back up the stairs to do what they'd been hired to do: pack up all clothes and household items and drop them off at the warehouse where they'd stay until they would be needed by victims of domestic violence.

Clancy, in the lead, crossed the threshold of the bedroom doorway and stopped short. Ben bumped into him. Dan bumped into Ben. "Come on you clowns. Get in there. Go. Move. Work."

The box Clancy had filled and taped shut near the dresser stood ripped open and empty. He turned around and pushed his way back to the living room.

Jenna stood at the open drawer, laden down with as

much of her jewelry—bracelets, rings, and necklaces—as she could wear so they couldn't steal that too. With forceful, deliberate movements, she folded a shirt and slapped it down on the pile of clothes she'd already put away.

When the drawer slammed shut, Ben bolted to the living room to stand with Clancy. "Tell me you didn't see that," he said to Dan.

Dan held onto the doorframe with a white-knuckled grip. "I don't see anything but empty boxes. And a bunch of clothes that need to get packed. Now, you two better get in here and get busy."

"No, you can't do this." Jenna let out a wail.

Patrick stuck his head through the door of their condo as Jenna flew past and down the stairs, yelling for Marvin.

Chapter 10

Each time he noticed TINA-I'll-be-your-server-today make a fresh pot of coffee, Tommy waited for it to finish dripping, grabbed it to fill their cups, and put the near empty pot back on the warmer. The fourth time it happened, Tina stood in front of the brewer, her hands balled into fists, whirled around and fumed, "All right. Who drained the pot again? You sons-of-bitches better quit serving yourselves. I swear to *God*—"

The deadheads roared with laughter.

Tina's arms dropped to her sides, her face screwed up in a ball, and she let out a mournful wail as the tears flowed.

Moe, the owner of the deli, ran out from the back of the restaurant to chastise her for offending the paying clientele and stopped short. There wasn't a customer to be seen. He went to Tina and helped her to a table. "Honey, are you okay? Maybe you better sit for a while, take it easy."

"I swear, Moe, that's the *tenth* time this morning. I make a fresh pot, turn my back, and it's empty again."

"Don't believe her," Dixon, one of Tommy's Sunday morning regulars, said. "It was only four." And the crowd of ghostly images laughed again.

Marvin heard Jenna yelling his name before he saw her burst through the glass door in a panic and jumped from his seat. "What? What's wrong?"

"You have to stop them. They're taking everything, *everything*."

"Whoa, whoa, slow down. What are you talking about?"

"There's a bunch of men and they're throwing things out, putting stuff into boxes. You have to stop them, Marvin." Jenna grabbed his arm and tried to pull him along. She'd about made it to the door before realizing excessive force caused her hand to slide right through his arm. Stopping and turning back to him, she implored, "Come on, Marvin, you have to help me." She ran back through the window adding an urgent, "Hurry."

Marv stuck his head through the glass to see which route home Jenna used and dropped his cup on the table. "I better go. I'll catch up with you guys later."

****

"Dude, we're right behind you." Tommy and Mike rushed out, leaving their cups on the table, the coffee sloshing over the rims.

Moe shook his head and looked at the table where three cups appeared out of nowhere. He took in a slow breath. *These guys are gonna be the death of me. And, if Tina quits, when I get there, I'm gonna give 'em all a piece of my mind.* He swiveled his chair around to keep the sight from Tina and offered in a soothing voice, "You want to go home and lie down for a while? I can handle things until the supper crowd."

Dixon grabbed the coffee cups the guys had left behind on their table and put them into the bus tray, swiped one of Tina's cloths from the wait station and wiped off the table.

Tina glanced around the room and heaved a sigh.

"I'm sorry Moe, it's just that…"

Moe patted her shoulder. "It's okay, honey. You just sit and relax. You want something to drink?"

Tina picked up a napkin, wiped her tears, and gave him a wan smile. "A stiff shot of something would be nice." Her eyes grew wide when he replied, "Coming right up."

He kept a bottle of bourbon stashed in his desk, put there soon after these types of things started to happen, which had been right after Tommy got shot in a late-night robbery of the deli. Moe had found him slumped on the floor in front of the safe, sitting in a pool of coagulated blood. Several weeks later, accusing her of stealing bagels and dumping gallons of good coffee down the drain, he'd fired the waitress. But other product, like corned beef, pastrami, knishes, continued to get mysteriously low. After a couple weeks, he accused the new girl of hiding stuff in the over-sized purse she lugged around. She'd grabbed her bag, flipped him the finger, and stomped out. The next morning, with his stock somehow replenished overnight, Moe, with a sheepish expression on his face, called to apologize and begged her to come back. She didn't, and he'd gone through countless waitresses over the years. But for some reason Tina clicked with him.

He returned to her with the bottle in his hand, wiping the dust from the neck and cap, opened it and set it on the table in front of her. "Here." After she'd taken a few swigs he asked, "Can I offer a little suggestion, honey?"

Tina sighed. "What the hell. Why not."

"The best thing you can do is not react to their shenanigans; ignore them. Go on about your business as if you don't see them happening."

Tina stared at him. "You mean you've seen—you knew—" Her voice softened with exhaustion and pain. "What the hell, Moe?"

"I'm sorry. I wasn't paying attention, wasn't thinking. I guess I'm just getting old." In fact, at the age of seventy-six, Moe had started mulling the idea of selling. Or out-and-out shutting down. Not that business had slacked off; just the opposite was true. Complaints were rare, and the crowds (living and dead) pressed against the walls waiting for a table to open. It became so hectic at times, he wondered how he and Tina managed to keep up.

Tina took another hit off the bourbon. "I thought I was going insane."

"His name is Tommy. He worked here, this was years ago." Moe glanced around the deli and sighed. "I think he loved this place more than me. I sure as hell wouldn't have taken a bullet for it."

Tina's back straightened, a frightened glaze swept into her eyes. "You mean he *died* in here?"

"I promise you, I've never met a sweeter kid. I think he just likes to have fun; he gets a kick out of messing with people."

"Well, it's not funny to me. It's creepy." Tina placed the bottle on the table with a bang, stood, and headed toward the back. "If he thinks he's gonna have fun at my expense—"

"Oh, God, you're not going to make me regret telling you, are you? It mostly only happens in the morning, you know that, right?" Moe liked her better than any other waitress he'd employed in the forty-five years he'd owned Epstein's. They meshed well and, over the two years she'd worked for him, he'd come to think of her as family. If she quit, he might as well sell. "I mean, you're not quitting on me, are you?"

Tina stopped and turned to him, a steely glint in her eyes, lips set in determination. "Quitting? No. We'll see who messes with who. Whom," she corrected herself.

"Then where're you going?"

"To fix my face. Then, I'm coming back in here and giving him a piece of my mind!" She stomped out of the room.

Chapter 11

The group returned to the condo to find JoAnne standing in the living room with her cell phone to her ear. Jenna's glum face brightened and she ran to her. "Jo. Thank God. You have to stop this. Don't let them take my things."

The four huddled around to listen in on JoAnne's conversation and Mike shouldered his way through her back. A shiver ran through her and she craned her neck for a view of the sliding door to the balcony. "Either there's a draft right here or those idiots opened a window."

She moved to the kitchen and leaned against the counter. Her unseen entourage went with her. "David? JoAnne. What's the problem? What happened? I thought you had this all arranged."

"I did. Why?"

"I came here to check on things, like you asked, and nothing's been done. Three guys are standing in the front of the building, with their thumbs up their asses, refusing to go back in." Except for loud hums and the banging of metal on metal, David's end of the line stayed silent. "David, are you there?"

"Yeah. Hold on a sec, it's too noisy here in the bakery. Let me go into the storeroom where I can talk...." The sounds of mixers and exhaust fans receded. "Okay, that's better. Now, what seems to be their problem?"

"Two of them are spouting some crazy bullshit."

"Like…"

"What difference does it make, David? I agreed to give you time to get through the holidays. It's the middle of February already. Now, this has to get done today. I have an appointment tomorrow with a consignment shop for the furniture and the rest of this shit needs to be gone."

Jenna turned to Marvin, confusion written in the creases of her forehead. "What is she saying, Marvin, what does this mean?"

Marvin ignored the question. "Shit? Did she say shit?" Marvin's hands balled into fists and he started in on one of his rants. "Did she just call our stuff shit? Doesn't she have some balls. How would she like it if we went into her place and—"

"Dude, calm down, it's just an expression."

Marvin raised his voice. "I'll give her an expression."

Jenna grabbed his arm. "Marv, shush. I want to hear what they're saying. I want to know what's happening."

JoAnne continued her conversation with David, oblivious to the ruckus going on around her.

Colleen, who had just walked in, wrapped an arm around Jenna's shoulder. "I thought I heard you all in here." Jenna allowed herself to be enveloped in a hug as Colleen continued. "What's wrong, dear? Patrick told me you ran out of the building, crying."

"I don't understand why they're boxing our things. They're putting them on a truck and—"

"Well, I hate to be the one to break it to you, dear.

But, it appears they're selling your things."

"But they can't. I need them." Jenna broke away from Colleen, a fresh torrent of tears welling up, and turned to Marvin.

Moving back into the living room, Mike shrugged. "Sorry, guys. But this is a fact of life. It's what happens when you die. Your belongings are given away. Besides, you can get whatever you need, any time you want."

Colleen gazed at Jenna with a sorrowful expression. "I know it's a shock to you, but I'm afraid he's right, dear. Besides, if you'll allow a foolish old woman her old-fashioned way of thinking, things are just things."

Jenna sniffled. "You're not foolish, don't talk like that."

"And, when the men are done in here," Colleen continued. "They'll be going across the hall to our place."

"Why would they do that?" Tommy wanted to know.

"Well, because—and I probably should've told her this before—it's because I left everything to her." Colleen nodded at Jenna.

Jenna stared in disbelief. "You did what?"

"Who else did Patrick and I have? And you were so kind to this old woman," Colleen said. Though the aches and pains and infirmaries of age had vanished with death, the habitual referral remained.

Jenna went to her. "Oh, that's so sweet."

"Oh, go on." Colleen gave a wave of her hand and smiled. Then she sighed and added, "Of course, now it'll go to whomever you named. Who *did* you leave your things to?"

Jenna pointed at JoAnne, who burst out in anger. "Have you lost your mind? I'm telling you, there's nobody here but me.... Fine. Whatever." She pulled the phone away from her ear and touched a finger to the screen. "Okay, you're on speaker, are you happy? Now what?"

David's voice came through clean and crisp. "Now, humor me. Don't interrupt, just stand and let me talk."

"I won't say a word. Talk 'til you're blue or your father grabs your ear and pulls you back to the ovens. Whatever makes you happy." JoAnne glared at the phone.

"Marv? You're there, aren't you? You said something about an expression?"

"You are one crazy motherfucker," JoAnne grumbled.

"You need to keep quiet, JoAnne, and let me talk."

"I'm not saying a word. You go right ahead and have your conversation with…" She gawked around the room. "The walls."

Marvin leaned over the phone in JoAnne's outstretched hand. "She's a bit of a pushy broad, but don't pay any attention to her, David." Jenna slapped Marvin. "Ow! You could let a guy finish. You never let me finish, Jen."

"I'll let you finish all right."

"Now, now, you two, don't start. Don't make your Uncle Tommy put you in separate corners."

"Look, Marv, and I assume Jenna and your two buddies that came to visit me last year are there, too."

Marv leaned over the phone again. "They are. And the woman from across the hall. I take it you know she left everything to Jenna."

"I know this is tough on you, both of you. But, it has to be done. The men are there because everything—clothes and household goods—are being given to the women's shelter you used to volunteer with, Jenna. Because I thought that's what you would want."

In awe that Marvin seemed to be having a conversation with his brother because the living never seemed to hear her when she spoke, Jenna nodded in silent agreement, but gave a questioning look to Tommy.

"Well, some people are open to it. David appears to be one of them. Eh, mostly it's kids. They haven't lost the ability to believe in things they can't see."

"Look, Marvin," David continued after a pause, "I don't know how things work over there—"

"Well, duh!" Tommy interjected and Mike shushed him.

"—so I'll just have to hope… Anyway, I'm happy you two are together. If she'd believe me, Ma would be thrilled."

Hearing that comment, Jenna's face screwed up into disbelief and she found her voice. "Oh, yeah, that'll be the day."

"But, at some point, the world has to move on. So, Jenna," David added, "let these guys do what they need to do. Deal?" He paused and strained to listen for a response.

Jenna's shoulders dropped in defeat. "I guess. What else can I do?"

"I miss you guys. Be good, okay? Oh, and Marv? Come visit again sometime, there's beer in the fridge just for you.… Okay, JoAnne, that should do it."

JoAnne heaved a sigh. "You are totally crackers, you know that? I think all that yeast has gone to your brain."

"Yeah, well. See if it doesn't help, then judge. Call if you need anything else."

"What are you going to do, bring in ghost hunters?" JoAnne taunted and shook her head.

Singing the theme to *Ghost Busters*, Tommy moved to her, gripped the edge of the phone with one hand, and tapped a finger against the screen.

JoAnne watched with a bored expression as the keyboard function activated and 'BOO!' appeared on the screen. "Yeah, that's funny, David. Look, I have to get back to the office. I'll talk to you later." She ended the call and walked out the door in search of the workmen.

Tommy looked at Jenna in surprise. "Dude, she's a tough cookie."

Jenna, who'd gotten used to Tommy addressing everyone as 'dude,' let loose a short chuckle. "Yes, she is. But, now what? Where do we all go?" She gestured to Marvin and Colleen.

"You move into the hotel," Mike said. "There're five more suites on our floor that rarely get booked."

"That's a great idea! Dudes, think of the fun we can have."

Jenna turned to Marvin, who nodded and said, "It is pretty swanky."

"Then it's settled?" Jenna turned to Colleen with a questioning look.

Colleen gazed at the group, one at a time in turn. "Why would you young people want such a couple of old fogeys hanging around?"

"Now, how can I live anywhere if you're not across the hall with your tea?"

Colleen turned wistful. "Well, I can't promise anything; I do have to consider Patrick again."

"Mrs. McClaskey?" Mike offered his arm to squire her back across the hall. "I'd be happy to talk to him about it."

"Where else do you have to go," Tommy inquired.

After taking Mike's proffered arm, Colleen turned to Tommy. "Patrick told me about…well, this may sound a bit odd but, then again, everything here seems odd, doesn't it? But, he told me about a woman, this amazing-sounding woman who offered to let him join her. He told her he had to wait for me. Wasn't that dear of him? Anyway, he said she was the most serene looking person he'd ever met, that there was something about her; a brightness, an aura around her that felt warm and inviting. And he'd like to find her to see if we might both go with her."

Tommy's face dropped into sadness. "Teresa. He means Teresa, doesn't he?"

"I believe that was her name, yes. Why the sullen look, young man? It sounded like heaven to me."

"That's it…" In answer to the questioning looks, Tommy explained, "But, once you join her, that's it."

"What does that mean, hippie?"

"Marvin, dude, she's Jason's, uh…" Tommy struggled for a moment. "Opposite, I guess you'd call it."

The conversation was interrupted when the three men returned, stepping into the room with slow, cautious steps. Dan, again taking up the rear and pushing his co-workers from behind, stopped half way through the room, shuddering with a sudden chill.

Colleen let out a little scream and jumped aside when Ben stumbled through her and she ran right through Clancy. He let out a yelp, ran to the bedroom, and slammed the door behind him, breathing hard.

Tommy laughed. "You think that can keep us out?" He strode to the door, pushed his head through and yelled, "Heeeeeere's Johnny." A loud scream emanated from the room. "Oh, my God! Did you hear that scream? Like a little girl. The dude shivered in a violent tremble, and went screaming and running to the other side of the room. You'd have thought he could actually see my head pop through his chest!" Tommy fell into a fit of giggles. "Good lord, these guys are priceless. I swear, I want to stay and mess with them all afternoon."

Dan crossed through the living room, barking orders. "When I open that door, I better not see anything but asses and elbows, and full boxes to carry out to the truck."

Jenna, who'd taken the full brunt of Dan as he walked through her, followed and slapped at him repeatedly. "I thought I told you to get out." Then she removed several costume jewelry bracelets and dropped them to the floor in front of his face. Turning back to the group, she smiled. "He deserved that."

Dan ignored the raining bracelets. In a series of gasps, he bent over double, clutching at his left arm. "Ah, shit. I think I'm having a heart attack." He forced some coughs, and plopped to the edge of Marvin's chair, rubbing at the numbness in his arm. "No, no, no. This can't be happening."

"Oh, don't worry, big boy." Mike picked up the errant jewelry, and patted Dan's shoulder. "The feeling will pass."

"My heavens, all this is too much commotion for my liking." Colleen headed through the entry. "I think I'd like a nice soothing cup of tea. Would anybody like to join me?"

Chapter 12

Jenna had long since realized it wasn't the tea itself that soothed her old friend, but the ritual of preparation. She pulled out Colleen's best china and silver tea service to set the table.

"Napkins and all, dear," Colleen said. "Just because we're…well, *here* doesn't mean we shouldn't follow proper procedure for entertaining guests," and she went about boiling the water and preparing the tea.

Marvin and Tommy ran to Epstein's where they snatched a half-dozen bagels from the bakery case.

Moe let out a sigh as they disappeared, one by one, into thin air. "Oh, of course. Don't forget the cream cheese," he said when the cooler door slid open. "God forbid you should leave my last container for a paying customer."

"Eh, go ahead, put it back," Marvin said, even as he gazed at the container with longing. "I think I can do without the *schmear*. I don't know where he gets it, but his is heads above the crap in the grocery stores."

"Up to you, dude." Tommy waited, holding the cooler open.

"The coolers aren't for augmenting the air conditioning, you know," Moe said in a huff under his breath, turning back to his grill.

"We might have some in the fridge. I'll check on the way back. And, if not, maybe Mrs. McClaskey has some."

Tommy shrugged and let the door slide closed.

****

Thirty minutes later, everyone had gathered around the dining table and Patrick passed the cups as Colleen poured.

"This is really nice, Colleen," Mike said accepting his.

Colleen smiled broadly. "It is, isn't it? I find a nice cup of tea does wonders. You know, I just realized, we haven't had this many people at our table in, goodness, how many years has it been, Patrick?"

Patrick passed a cup over to Marvin. "Oh, let me calculate. I retired in, what, nineteen…eighty-seven."

"Eighty-six," Colleen corrected.

"And we hosted a small gathering that Christmas just before I crossed over. So, that's, my goodness." Patrick's eyes opened wide. "It's been twenty-eight years."

Tommy accepted his cup. "Oh, dude, you'd just retired? Isn't that a total bummer?"

Patrick smiled at him. "It is indeed a 'total bummer'. But only because it meant being parted from my beautiful lassie, here."

Colleen blushed and gave a small wave of her hand. "Oh, go on with you."

"Oh, let him, Colleen." Marvin hoisted his cup in a toast. "I know exactly what he means."

She placed a hand to her chin as if to shield her comment, though her volume didn't lower a bit. "I fully intend to, Marvin. But a girl has to play the proper role, you know." After the laughter settled, she took her place at the end of the table opposite her husband and prompted the conversation. It wouldn't do to have awkward moments of silence. A hostess' duty to lead conversation and see to her guests comfort was one of the things she believed in. "Now, Tommy, you were beginning to tell us all about this Teresa before you were so abruptly cut short."

"Oh, right." Tommy put his cup on the table and grew oddly serious. "Um, how do I explain this? She, Teresa that is, is the head of a sect here. When you, um…"

"Die," Marv blurted out.

Tommy scowled. "Dude, don't be so crass. We don't need to upset the folks who are new here."

"It's quite all right," Colleen assured him. "No one needs to walk on egg shells."

Tommy nodded. "Anyway, these groups know how we've lead our lives." He put a hand up to Mike's questioning look. "How I couldn't tell you, but they know. Just like Jason and his people know who shouldn't be allowed here and take them right away so they can't do any more bad things. But, with Teresa's group, an offer is made; we have a choice. We can stay here or join them."

"Is the choice final?" Patrick's brow creased.

"To stay here, no. In fact, lots of people, usually older ones like you," Tommy said, nodding to his hosts. "They just get, I don't know, tired I suppose is the right word, and they go. I've seen it happen. There's this pure, bright white aura that grows around them—these Sanctuarians, I guess you might call them, they don't really have a name that I know of—and they get huge. Just like Jason did with you Marv, but it's not scary or anything. Then their bodies just sort of surround the person, they shrink back down to normal size and, poof!

"But once you accept and go into them, you can't come back here. I guess that's why the world isn't overrun with us," Tommy concluded.

"What happens? In them, I mean," Jenna's voice came out a quiet whisper.

"I don't know." Tommy shrugged. "I've heard rumors, of course, that everything is wiped clean, your memory, everything; like you never existed." His body shuddered. "The claim is, it's what Hindus refer to as 'Bardo,' where people are prepared for rebirth." Colleen and Patrick exchanged a glance and a sense of worried urgency entered Tommy's voice. "You aren't thinking of going, are you? Oh, you can't, you just can't. Tell me you aren't ready to do that, yet."

"Tommy!" Mike nudged him. "Don't you think that's up to them?"

"But they can't. I mean, they have to stay. At least until after the wedding."

A chorus of jumbled words filled the air, as everyone spoke at once, until Jenna stood and her volume overpowered the rest. "Stop, already."

"Jenna, dear, but I think it's wonderful! And, Tommy, we grant your wish." Colleen shifted her focus to her husband. "Don't we, Patrick?"

Enthusiastic nods from the guests accompanied his response. "If that's what you want to do, that's what we'll do."

"You see, Marvin?" Jenna asked, her hands on her hips.

Marvin looked around in confusion. "See what?"

"Why can't you be that cooperative?" Jenna

stabbed a finger in his direction.

"What are you talking about?" Marvin dropped his bagel onto the plate, and stood causing his napkin to slide from his lap to the floor. "I'm cooperative, I'm always cooperative."

"Oh, yeah, right." Jenna taunted as he bent over to retrieve his errant napkin issuing an exasperated sigh. "It's always what you want. What about—"

"Now, now, children, what has your Uncle Tommy told you two about arguing in front of company?" Tommy stood and his arms stretched wide. "I think we need a hug!"

"Oh, give it rest, hippie," Marvin said, but smiled.

Jenna broke out in laughter. "But, he's being mean to me, Uncle Tommy."

"There, there, don't you worry. I'll straighten him out." Tommy launched around the room toward Marvin, his arms thrown wide. Laughing, Marvin beat him off.

Patrick, on to the fun from the beginning, asked, "You want me to take him out behind the shed, Tommy? I'm sure I can find a nice hickory switch." He winked at Marvin.

"That's just what my father used to threaten. Except we didn't have a shed."

"But I'll bet he had the switch though, didn't he?"

"Boy, did he ever. And one hell of a swing," Marvin replied.

The group was raucous with laughter when Diane's voice carried through the din. "Helloooo. Jenna? Where are you?"

"In here," Jenna called out. She embraced Diane in air kisses with a pained expression. "With all the commotion of our place being emptied out, I completely forgot we planned a shopping trip."

Diane gave a disdainful glance at Jenna's attire. "It does appear you need something, uh, new, shall we say." A smile broke across her face. "Well, then, it's fortuitous we're going shopping, isn't it? I'm ready anytime you are."

"Well, pardon me, but I didn't think we were headed to Rodeo Drive."

"I think she looks quite lovely," Colleen said with a hint of dislike and a glare for the woman who'd burst uninvited into her dining room. Don't make disparaging remarks and you'll be treated with respect is a motto she lived by.

Jenna laughed. "Colleen, I believe you might be a tad bit biased. Colleen, this is Diane; Diane, our neighbors, Colleen and Patrick. Colleen was a godsend after Marvin passed. Honestly, I don't know what I would've done without her."

Diane shook hands with Colleen in a firm grip and said nothing, then held her hand out for Patrick, who stood, and gave a slight bow as he kissed the back of it. "Well, it's a pleasure." She turned to Jenna. "Shall we go, then?"

Jenna hesitated, her brow knit with indecision.

"You go on with your friend, dear, and enjoy yourself. I think it'll do you good. Take your mind off things, so to speak," Colleen offered. "We'll catch up later."

Marvin waved in agreement. "Yeah, go. Come find us at the hotel, top floor. These two knuckleheads will help move some things over, so it won't feel completely foreign."

"Far out, dudes." Tommy broke out in a wide smile. "Our own little commune."

Chapter 13

Jenna and Diane didn't get far into their excursion. After stopping at a few stores for Diane, who claimed she needed to check some things, they headed for the main thoroughfare and a bus to take them to the mall. Loud screaming emanated from the same alleyway as the morning of Jenna's funeral. She halted in disbelief at the number of people who walked past without even a glance. Those who did look quickened their pace as if they were afraid the attacker might come after them. "Are you kidding me? Are you people deaf? What is wrong with you? Has everyone in the world turned into a coward, afraid to get involved?"

Diane stopped and turned around. "What are you going on about?"

"Tell me you don't hear that woman." Jenna pointed into the alleyway. She looked around at the number of deadheads in the vicinity. "How can you all just stand here and watch some poor woman get beaten?"

"There's nothing we can do about it," one retorted.

"He's right." Diane shrugged. "Besides, the living really aren't our concern. Why should we care about what those people do?"

"Bullshit! There's plenty we can do." Jenna, not understanding why it shouldn't be everyone's concern, stormed down the passageway. Half way to the fighting couple, she realized it wasn't only the same location, it was the same man beating the same woman. From her years of volunteer work at the shelter, it didn't surprise her but her anger flared. She ran at the man, lunged at his mid-section like a tight-end tackle, and skidded along the asphalt. The rough pavement shredded small holes into her clothing. The guy continued to pummel the girl's head.

"It's your own fault. Why do you make me do this, Kate? Huh? How many times do I have to tell you to shut your trap?" With each sentence, the man landed another punch.

Jenna muttered, "What the hell?" It took her a moment to realize why the slaps she'd landed on the mover earlier in the day had an effect when this idiot didn't flinch. She concentrated on checking the blow upon contact so her foot wouldn't fly right through his body. She stood directly behind him and aimed a swift kick squarely between his spread legs. He howled, grabbed his groin, and dropped to the pavement.

Kate stood in shock, her hands covering her mouth at the sight. "Oh shit, Harvey. What the hell happened?" Her husband glared at her and she pushed herself against the wall, one hand outstretched. "I didn't do it, Harv. I didn't do nothin', I swear."

Jenna moved to her right and kicked him in the face.

"Jenna! What are you doing? Stop it. You can't do this." Diane stood fifteen feet away, an air of high society, I'm-above-it-all in her posture.

"You want to bet?" Jenna asked. "If you had any decency, you'd be over here helping me instead of standing there like some debutante afraid a hair might shift out of place."

Harvey rocked himself on the hard ground, and checked his nose for blood. The bellow that roared from him startled his wife. She leaned down to him. "Oh, my God, Harvey, are you all right?"

He rose and lunged at her. "You bitch, you think you can kick me in the balls and get away with it?" He grabbed her arm and threw her into the side of the building. The crack of a bone resounded beneath the air that expelled from the woman's lungs.

"Help me!" came to Diane's ears from the living and the dead, and she moved closer.

Afraid the woman's chance would pass, Jenna grabbed at the woman in a panic but her hand swiped through each time. "Run. Will you get away from him before he kills you?" A sudden fear manifested itself across Jenna's brow. "Oh, God!" She turned her attention to the man again. Her hands clawed at his coat pockets, looking for the gun he'd threatened to use during the previous altercation. "I can't tell. Shit, I can't tell."

"Can't tell what?" Diane asked, still standing off to one side of the fracas.

Jenna glared in desperation. "The gun. At least help me get the gun."

Jason stood across the street from the farthest end of the alley and watched, but made no move. He knew there was no gun this time, and there would be no possibility of real harm to the living. Still, he shook his head in sadness. "You's gon be a handful, I can see that fo' sho'. I know you's tryin' to he'p, but you best be watchin' yo' step."

"Oh, for crying out loud. Let me show you how to

disarm a man." Diane walked warily to avoid punches, ran her hand into his crotch and squeezed. An icy jolt shot up through his body, his head jerked up, and he howled in pain. She followed and held on as he moved to plant his back against the brick building.

"Ow, ow, ow. What the hell?" He unbuttoned his jeans and dropped them to his ankles. He looked down and pawed at the pain. Diane kept a firm grip on him. "What the hell is this? Holy shit, my balls are on fire, like they're in an ice-cold vise."

Diane let up a bit on the pressure. Harvey cupped his groin, gulping deep breaths of air.

"Harvey? Harvey, should I call someone?" Kate asked and shuffled things around in her purse looking for her phone. "Does it still hurt?"

"What do you think, you stupid bitch?" He glared at her and raised a fist. Diane clamped down again. Harvey's eyes squinted shut. "Motherfucker."

Jenna turned toward the sound of her name to see Marvin, Tommy, and Mike sprinting down the alley, laden with boxes and bags. Marvin scowled at her. She stood like a wrestler in the ring challenging an opponent, and asked, "What, Marv?"

He peered nervously at each end of the narrow passage, but the moving masses between them kept Jason from his view. "What are you doing? You're cruising for trouble. You've already been warned about this."

"Well, what do you expect me to do, Marvin? You know I can't just ignore it. So, you tell me, what am I supposed to do?"

Marvin's expression grew soft. "Look, kiddo, I know it kills you but you can't do this. You can't interfere."

"I can't not interfere."

Diane glanced around and asked, "Should I let him go?"

Mike nodded. "Probably better."

She gave a strong squashing compression, smiled at hearing one last yelp of pain, and let go. "That's too bad. I kind of liked that."

As soon as the pressure let up, Harvey exhaled a long relieved breath and cupped his testicles. "Oh, holy crap."

Ignoring her own pain, Kate ran a hand up and down his forearm in sympathy. "Did it stop, sweetie? Are you better now?"

"Yeah."

With nervous glances at the people walking past the ends of the alley, Katie said, "You better pull your pants up, Harv. What if a cop sees you standing here, groping yourself like that?"

He stood rubbing gently at his groin. "Fuck 'em. My nuts are killin' me."

"You could be right." Diane chuckled at him. "You might want to go get those checked, they didn't feel quite right to me. But, then again, it has been a long time," she admitted with a wistful sigh.

A young man walking by noticed and stopped. Laughing, he raised his cell phone, snapped a picture, and went on his way.

Kate stepped over to shield Harvey from the view of the street. "Jesus, Harvey, pull your pants up. People are looking."

Harvey leaned around her and flipped up a middle finger. "I don't care. Now shut up."

"Well, maybe I do."

"I told you to shut your mouth." He swung a backhand across her face.

"This guy just doesn't learn." Jenna, ready to swing, started toward Harvey.

"Jenn, no!" Marvin dropped the parcels from his grasp and lunged to step between the two. He lost his footing and his eyes opened wide in surprise when he fell into Harvey. Struggling to break free, Marvin shouted for help but the words were muffled at first. "You know, I've felt people walk through me, I've bumped through others, but never been there longer than a millisecond. This is the weirdest sensation I've ever experienced. And, worse, I can read the guy's thoughts and this is not a nice man! Can somebody please get me out of him?"

Harvey began a wild spastic dance, arms twitching, legs bending, head bobbing and jerking around, all in different directions. His mop of dirty hair swirled around his head. His face contorted and convulsed into new features, blurring into one as the two men tried to untangle their mingled entities. He shouted a string of obscenities. Kate, again plastered against the building in fear, understood the cusswords, but the rest was a jumble of sounds. The deadheads understood it all.

While the rest of the gang panicked and grabbed at limbs to pull them apart, Tommy began to laugh. "Oh, my God, dude. You should see yourself, Marvin," he sputtered through giggles, and mimicked the movements. "Oh, my God. Oh, my God, this is hysterical." He turned away in an attempt to control himself, but as soon as his gaze fell on the puppetry again he broke into another fit. "This is funnier than when you electrocuted yourself with Jenna's hair dryer. Marv, dude, you better get out of there or I'm going to pee my pants."

As Harvey's body bent over, Marvin jerked upright. It took a second before he realized he'd broken at least partially free and stood frozen in place. For his friends, the effect was like some kind of magic trick: half man, half ghostly image. He reached out and took hold of Jenna's hand, stepped away, and the twitching Harvey fell to the ground in a silent heap. Kate rushed to him and, using her good arm, tugged at the pants still around his ankles.

"Holy mother of Mary!" Marvin turned around to study the body he'd just occupied.

Tommy was still struggling to get a grip on his fit of laughter. "Oh, man, that was priceless."

Marvin scowled and rushed at him. "I'll give you priceless, hippie."

Tommy bolted. Marvin gave chase but, as he did, he couldn't fight off Tommy's infectious giggles, and the others heard his laughter start. Mike called out, "Come on, you two, that can wait. Let's get out of here."

"Tha's a mighty fine idea," Jason said. He pushed away from the wall of the storefront he'd been leaning on. To avoid being detected by them, he walked over one alley and cut down to the next street to wait.

"Here, take these," Tommy said, pushing a load of packages at Diane, who opened her mouth to argue but shrugged and accepted them. While Marvin retrieved the things he'd dropped, Tommy wrapped an arm around Jenna's waist, and led the way toward the adjoining street. "Seriously, though, you need to stop doing that."

"But—"

"No buts, we aren't supposed to get involved, Jenna," Mike said.

"Come on, you guys." Jenna gave no indication that her wheels had already begun spinning based on Marvin's mishap. "There has to be something we can do."

"Don't worry. If it's that important, we'll think of something, won't we, Tommy?"

"Oh, you know it, Mike. But, first, we need to get this stuff to your new home and get you settled in."

Marvin stood on the sidewalk at the corner of the building and motioned with the stack in his hands. "The bus is almost to the stop. We better move fast. There's only three people waiting to get on. I don't relish the thought of running with all this stuff and trying to jump in."

Lagging behind, Diane asked, "Where are we going with all this?"

Jenna stopped to wait. "To a hotel. Where do you live?"

"With my ex-husband."

"Your ex? Why?"

"Oh, it's great. Really," Diane added for Jenna's questioning expression, and shoved everything into her arms. "The place is huge, there's more than enough room, every amenity I could ask for, and the fact the cheap bastard is still supporting me even though he doesn't know it is icing on the cake. And, messing with his mind on a daily basis is the cherry on top." She threw back her head and let loose with a loud, bright laugh.

"Come by sometime and I'll give you a tour," she said. After taking a minute to consider the new friends, she extended the invitation. "Better yet, you should all come. Spend the weekend. We can break into his stash of caviar, eat his lobster and filet mignon, go into the cellar and break open a bottle of his prized wine, and we'll top that off by drinking all his Louie."

The group emerged from between the buildings and boarded the bus. Jason nodded, satisfied that, at least for the time being, he could place his focus elsewhere.

Chapter 14

Dressed in a hotel bathrobe, Jenna dropped onto the sofa of the suite they'd commandeered and pointed to the tattered garments she'd removed. "Look at them. What a mess. You know, Marv, I can't believe you didn't at least grab a few of my clothes."

"Hey, I got your jewelry box, your make-up case, and all the ridiculous hair product and gadgets you use. So, we didn't get a couple blouses and skirts. Sue me," Marv replied, pouring two glasses of wine. "I got the important stuff. Besides, all you have to do is go see Davy and he'll help you pick out some new things."

"Important stuff. Important to you, maybe. As usual. You know, you could think about someone else for a change."

Marvin pushed a glass at her. "Oh, stuff it."

Jenna took the glass and hoisted it in a half-hearted toast. "I'll stuff it all right."

"Listen, stop feeling sorry for yourself."

"Stop being a prick, Marvin. You've been here a while. Well, not here, but you know what I mean. After the day I've had, I really didn't want to go out tonight. I just wanted to sit and try to get used to being homeless."

Though he wanted to tell her to stop being dramatic, Marvin hated it when she was sad and tried to find something that would make her feel better.

Standing at the sliding door to the terrace, he raised his glass. "What do you call this? It's a hell of a lot more swanky than the condo. Just look at this view. All the lights across the city, the stars up there. It's beautiful."

Jenna went to his side. "Yeah, but it's not ours, Marv."

He switched his glass to the other hand to accommodate her, draped an arm across her shoulders, and pulled her close. "I know, kiddo. But, you'll get used to it. The toughest part is when someone books the place, which according to Mike isn't very often. I guess visiting dignitaries for the Air Force base aren't as plentiful these days. Anyway, other than that, the occasional maid makes a cursory sweep through. You can pretty much do what you want."

They stood silent, alone in their thoughts for the longest time, staring out at the night.

"Hello?" Tommy's voice broke in.

They both turned at the sound of his voice and Jenna laughed. All that was visible was Tommy's head poking through the middle of the door. "You look like some door knocker out of a Dickens novel."

"Come on in, hippie! Have a glass of wine with us. Where's Mike?"

"Eh, watching some lame program on Animal Planet," Tommy said, fading through the door. "Boring. I tried to get him to charge a movie to the room, but he won't do it. Said we've already done that too much and he doesn't want to take advantage since the hotel eats the cost in the end."

"I'm afraid it's not much more exciting here."

"Anyway, I was thinking—"

"Uh-oh. You gotta be careful when he says that,"

Marv warned Jenna.

"Dude! No, I know how you hate shopping and thought if Jenna wanted to go get some clothes I'd go with her. I seriously cannot sit and watch salmon spawn while some actor drones on about it without any vocal inflection. I'd rather get a hundred noogies from you."

Marv chuckled and headed toward him. "I can accommodate that."

Tommy put a hand out to stop him. "Dude, that was a hypothetical noogie. What do you say, Jenna? Davy is always a kick in the pants."

Jenna waited for Marvin to shrug his indifference. "Okay, let me take off the robe, which is quite comfy I have to admit, and put the ruined clothes back on. It'll just take a minute."

"Far out!"

"What will you do, Marvin?" Jenna's voice filtered from the bedroom.

"I don't know. Maybe I'll go watch fish spawn with Mike," he replied to goad Tommy's expression of distaste.

****

Jenna and Tommy managed to catch the last bus of the evening that would take them to an empty Nordstrom. Well, empty of live people, anyway; as was usual at night, the place would be crawling with deadheads. On their walk across the parking lot, Tommy asked, "So, what're you thinking?"

"I don't know. Maybe a pair of nice jeans." Jenna considered her options. If she got into any more skirmishes, and she undoubtedly would—she wasn't about to give up no matter what Nancy or this Jason (whoever he was) said—denim would hold up better than the ruined cotton skirt and silk blouse she had on. "And I'm thinking maybe a man's flannel shirt."

"Well, Davy is sure to find the perfect match. Hey, we could get a really cool sweatshirt to pull over it all, too."

Jenna shrugged. "We'll see."

Inside the store, ignoring the concerned expressions of passers-by, they headed for the men's section which was Davy's usual nighttime haunt. Tommy peered over the racks of clothes, Jenna scoured between them, and found no sign of their favorite clothier. They met at the very back of the store next to the fitting rooms.

"Nope," Jenna confirmed.

"Maybe he's in helping somebody. Hold on a sec." Tommy brushed through the curtain, searched each room, and returned with a shake of his head.

"Guess we're on our own."

"Can I help you find something?" A man rounded a rack of casual shirts.

"More like someone," Tommy replied. "Have you seen Davy around?"

The man frowned. "Davy. Everyone wants Davy."

"Sorry, dude. No offense, really. It's just that—"

The guy waved off the apology. "Sure, sure. He's out of town."

"Really?" Jenna asked. "Where'd he go?"

"Miami. Ha!" He rolled his eyes. "He thinks he's going to meet Versace."

Tommy laughed. "Well, I gotta say, if anyone can pull off getting to someone like that, it would be Davy."

"Yeah, yeah. Whatever." The man wandered away.

"Well, I really didn't need help anyway. May as

well get started. Jeans, first," Jenna stated, and turned to head for the women's department.

A pair of dark gray Levi's looked good and fit well, she wandered to the young men's racks, and shuffled through long sleeved shirts until settling on one in a medium tan.

"Yeah, cool, that one's good. Lets your hair color stand out," Tommy offered. "Now what?"

Perusing the signage, Jenna spotted her next stop and pointed. "That way. Something comfortable, and sturdy," she said, making her way to the shoes.

She took her time walking the aisles, gazing at the shelves top to bottom, when a pair of tan boots caught her eye. She pulled the box and sat on a bench to try them on. "Crap. I need socks. Tommy, grab a pair from the shelf over there, please."

Tommy tore the wrapper off, handed them to her, and waited. "And?"

"They're a bit snug, but they'll stretch, right?"

"Hey, if they don't have a larger size on the shelf, we can always go into the back and tear the place apart. It'll give the day shift something to do tomorrow."

Jenna stood and took a few steps, turned and came back with a smile. "No, I think I can make these work."

"Are you sure? It's a long walk back."

"Eh, so if they start to hurt, I'll take them off and go barefoot."

"Your feet'll get cold," Tommy warned.

"Like they aren't perpetually cold now."

Tommy laughed. "Yeah, well, I guess you've got a point there, dude."

Chapter 15

Davy wasn't in any rush. The plan took weeks to figure out, but there he was in Miami. Ignoring the buzz as he pushed through people on the trek up the gangway from the plane to the terminal, his anticipation and excitement peaked. Inside the airport he paused long enough to locate the signs for Ground Transportation. The cabs would keep running, especially during the high season of travel to the warmer climate, but he sprinted along the concourse.

He stood and waited until a voice said, "South Beach," then jumped into the back seat and had settled in for the ride before the driver slammed the trunk closed over her passenger's luggage. His mounting excitement so overwhelmed him, and his mind raced with ideas as the scenery rushed by, that he gave little more than a passing glance—the slightest disdainful wrinkle of the nose—to the so-last-collection ensemble of his fellow passenger.

At the Cardoza Hotel, Davy pushed through the cab door rather than startle his unknowing hosts by opening and slamming it shut. He consulted the tourist map he'd snatched from a rack on his way through the airport, established his bearings, and headed south the few blocks to the now-infamous villa on Ocean Drive, the former Casa Casuarina. At two-forty-five in the morning, the huge wrought iron gates were closed, of course, as were the double doors to what now served as the lobby to a hotel since the designer's murder.

Once inside, Davy paused to take in the grandeur of the ornate palace and sighed. The building was much larger than pictures of the front façade might lead one to believe. "This could be a long hunt. But I know you've got to be here somewhere. I'd bet my reputation on it. Now," he played out a silent eeny-meeny-miney-moe at the cascading windows along the back, the staircase, and various hallways leading off in different directions and cooed, "Giaaaneee. Where are you? Come out, come out, wherever you are."

"Don't be ridiculous," a voice echoed through the room. "What do you want?"

Davy turned full circle in search of the owner of the decidedly male voice. "Hello?"

A hand popped up over the back of a sofa and waved. As Davy made his way across the expanse, the man himself sat upright. Though Davy longed to flap his hands through the air and his insides screamed, "Oh, my God, oh, my God," he managed to contain himself. The only outward excitement he allowed was a huge, white-toothed smile that exploded over his face, an outstretched hand in greeting, and the steps he took much too fast. "Mr. Versace, sir," he babbled, crossing the room. "I don't know, I feel like I should bow or something."

True to his fashion sense, Versace was dressed for the climate in linen pants and shirt and sandals. Perhaps because of the manner in which he'd died, the ordinarily personable man had become wary of strangers. Gianni acknowledged the outstretched hand but didn't offer his own. "You are?"

"Oh, uh, David. David Krauss. Davy."

"Uh, huh. And."

Davy finally allowed his hand to drop down to his side and the smile lessened. It always hurt his feelings when famous people acted as if it pained them to have to deal with peons, mere mortals of the world. *As if.* Yet he was determined to succeed in this quest. "I'd like you to design a dress."

The great man chuckled. "In case you hadn't noticed, I've been involuntarily retired."

"Well, you'll want to un-retire for this. I promise."

"I can't imagine." Versace gave a bored gesture toward a chair. "But, go on."

Davy sat and opened the large manila envelope he'd clutched for the past six hours. With an almost religious reverence he slid a photo out and handed it over. "Can you imagine designing a wedding gown for her?"

Davy had stolen the photo of Jenna while he knew nobody was home. Taken at a picnic of some sort, the picture didn't immediately impress, it took a moment. "These are not the legs of a model, no." Versace tapped a fingernail to the print as he lectured. "The hips and waist have good proportions. The breasts, mmm, a little large, but nice, shall we say? The neckline is good." His studied gaze moved up to the face and he paused for a long moment. "This *señorina*, this woman, she's—" He placed fingers to his mouth and tossed a kiss to the air. "Is it her eyes? Or, perhaps her smile? But, there's a look, a how do you say? An aura."

Davy nodded. "It's going to be a wedding for the ages. This will top anything you've ever seen or heard about. So, of course, I knew you had to be the one to do this."

"And, this *señorina*, she would be *a proprio agio*, eh, comfortable, with one such as I, she wouldn't be frightened?"

"Oh, heavens, no." Davy relaxed more into his usual sense of self and added, "Honey, she's as dead as we are."

"Really." Gianni gazed at the picture. "And you say she's getting married? Is this possible?"

Davy straightened in his chair. "Who's going to stop it? I intend to make this the most fabulous event ever. Di's wedding will seem positively pauperish in comparison."

Gianni stood. "Well, I must think about this. There's an empty room." He pointed to the ceiling, sighed, and said with an undertone of disgust, "A hotel. It's disturbing, what they've done with my home. But, we learn to…live, I suppose." He paused for another sorrowful sigh as he glanced around what used to be his own living room. "So, you must go and rest. Meet me in the morning, shall we say nine o'clock? We'll help ourselves to what they pass off as coffee, and I'll render my decision."

Davy had never experienced such a long few hours in his life. This wait was worse than some wakes he'd attended over the years. Ones that felt weeks long, as he listened to mourner after mourner drone on for days about how wonderful, what a good father, brother, son, nephew, friend the deceased had been, until he screamed for them to "Shut. Up. Already. Lord have mercy." Not that the bereaved heard him, but fellow deadheads and, more often than not, even the recently departed appreciated the gesture.

Before the appointed meeting time the next morning, Davy sat fidgeting in a chair in the lobby, like a five-year-old in anticipation of his turn at the piñata, and waited. And waited. An hour passed and still no sign of Versace. Davy wandered through the building and followed his nose to the solarium, now the hotel restaurant, and there the designer sat, tapping a thumb against the table in irritation at being kept waiting. Davy rushed to the table. "Please, accept my apologies. I thought you meant—"

Versace held up a hand to halt the excuses. "No. No excuses. Allow me to say, my new friend, this will not be acceptable. You're lucky I find this woman to be so irresistible. Otherwise you would be going back to—where is it?"

"Dayton."

Versace gave a single wave of dismissal. "Yes, yes, to Dayton. *Alone*. Now, I must meet her. And measure, of course. Then I must go to Paris for fabric and then Milan to build."

Unable to restrain himself, Davy's fearful expression broke into laughter. "Oh, my God, you'll do it? You're going to do it. I knew it. I knew you wouldn't be able to resist. Oh, this is fabulous!" His hands flapped at the air like he was attempting to ward off a hot flash.

Gianni observed Davy's state of excitement with an air of boredom. "Must we, really?"

Chapter 16

The whole wedding issue began to grate on Jenna's nerves and her mood turned surly. Whenever the opportunity presented itself, she walked through the city alone. The excursions became as much an effort to test her theory as an attempt to avoid Davy, who she'd been told was looking for her to go over some ridiculous plan.

She wandered up and down the streets, and repeatedly passed the alley of her previous altercations. When each inspection came up empty, she began to think maybe her hunch was right on the money; perhaps the man got so freaked out from the experience he'd mended his ways. Jenna realized it had been Marvin jumping into the mix that had saved the girl and provided her theory. Yet, the thought she'd actually helped someone boosted her spirits and emboldened her to give it a try.

In search of a test subject, she began to look at people with a new perspective. While sitting at Epstein's, she'd stolen peeks at Tina-I'll-Be-Your-Server-Today until Tommy noticed. Though they all perceived a shift in the waitress' attitude and demeanor over the past week, Tommy gave Jenna a scowl and slight shake of the head as if to say, "Not her. She couldn't handle it. You'd send her right over the edge."

Now, a woman about the same size and build as

99

Jenna stood at the bus stop tapping a finger to the screen of her cell phone, unaware of the ogling she got from a young man sitting on the bench behind her. Jenna walked over, looked each way down the street as if preparing to cross, pushed an arm into her, and felt the buzz of contact with the living. The woman shivered and grabbed the lapels of her jacket closed, but otherwise made no indication anything could be amiss. Jenna pushed until she had a full leg and arm embedded. The woman shifted her weight to the opposite leg, but other than issuing an offhand, muffled, "Lord, it's getting cold," continued with her obsession of the video game she'd been playing to pass the time.

Jenna again checked for reactions from deadheads in the area, but none appeared to pay the slightest bit of attention.

She pushed her way in and became disoriented for a second. The woman's head shook in confusion, her eyes squeezing shut, opening and peering across the street as if trying to refocus blurry vision. After a moment, she went back to the game on her phone. Using all the energy she could, Jenna slowly turned her head and raised her gaze. The man on the bench came into view. The woman's thoughts shifted into a question, *what am I looking at him for?* Jenna returned focus to the cell phone and the girl's thought pattern went right back to the shifting icons on the screen. Jenna raised a hand to scratch the back of her head, the woman's body followed suit. Jenna smiled and a smile spread across the woman's lips.

"Okay, now can I get out?" Jenna asked.

The woman gaped around, confused by the question that came out of her mouth, and surprised at the odd sound of her own voice.

"Get out of what?" a male voice behind her asked.

Jenna jerked around in surprise, but this time her host body didn't follow, and she stepped away.

"Oh, uh, I was just commenting on the game," the woman replied, lowered her voice and added, "I think." Then she expelled a breath of air, opened the buttons of her jacket, and mumbled, "What is with this weather?"

Jenna moved along the street, head high, in purposeful strides, but stopped every few blocks and tried out her new skills. The initial disorientation dissipated faster and the buzzing became less of a distraction. Each time it became easier to control the movements of the women she pushed into.

Nine tries from the first attempt, Jenna slipped in and, without so much as a second's hesitation, made the woman she'd taken over walk at a rapid pace. She pushed her way through a crowd, stepped to a counter at a coffee shop and placed an order, paid with cash from the woman's purse, took the steaming cup out to the street and removed herself. Not a single questioning thought broke through to Jenna's mind.

The woman stood quiet, looking from the cup in her hand to the store front, then shrugged and sipped at it as she returned the way she'd come.

"I think that's going do it." Jenna nodded in satisfaction and headed for the hotel.

Chapter 17

Jason watched with interest from his vantage point on the roof of a two-story building. He'd been able to focus on other issues until he became fully aware of Jenna's intent to disobey. Like all deadheads, he was quite familiar with the gag of the dead entering the bodies of the living. Most did it to mess with pseudo-psychics as a way to tease them or scare them out of preying on the innocent, or the grieving who were looking for reassurances their loved ones had crossed safely and were at peace. Like Marvin's brother, David, though his ability was weak, real mediums had no need of parlor tricks. They could converse easily with the dead.

But it was clear to Jason that Jenna had different intentions. He had no doubt she could slip in, no doubt she could extract herself. Despite Marvin's panicked machinations, that was the easy part. But how strong was she? Could she take control without doing harm?

Jenna walked down the street, head high, in purposeful strides. "It's gon' take you some practice, I see. But I got a feelin' you's just strong enough, and determined enough, to do it. Yep, you's gon' be a real handful, you is," he uttered in a quiet voice and followed.

Yet, the smile on her face disturbed him. "You's stronger than I thought." He turned his mind to his protégé, *you better come watch her*—His head jerked upright and a fierce, terrifying gleam glazed over his eyes. The spine straightened, eyes peered into the distance, and the appearance of the shuffling old man disintegrated. He finished his command to Nancy, *now!* and his form dissipated from view of any deadhead who may have been within eyesight.

Two miles away, Kate huddled between a nightstand and the wall to the bathroom of a rundown flophouse, her forearm still in a cast, and pleading voice rising in volume and pitch. Jason didn't have time to wonder why Harvey waved a gun around in a drunken rant when one had been taken from him during the previous altercation and left in a dumpster. Harvey's slurred obscenities came at the top of his lungs until a loud explosion in the tiny space pierced through his yelling. He dropped to the floor in a heap and Kate wailed.

Jason stood inside the closed door of the room and called to him, his deep bass voice booming through Harvey's ears. "Harvey."

Harvey stood up and gawked around. "What happened?" He glanced down at the body lying on the floor, the face a mangled mess, a pattern of black powder burns spread across one cheek. Blood oozed from the wound, drooled down the lower jaw and dripped onto the worn, threadbare carpeting.

"Harvey, you come over here now," penetrated his brain. Stunned, he looked toward Jason and screamed.

Jason's countenance stood huge and dark, his eyes big and deeper than any cave. With each unwanted step he took, Jason appeared to grow taller and spread wider, until Harvey was engulfed, swallowed as if he'd been sucked into a black hole in space.

Mournful, grieving howls pounded against Harvey's ears. Arms with crawling, grasping fingers clawed at him and pulled him into a bottomless well of pain and anguish. Tortured faces painted with evil smiles swam up at him. No matter how he struggled to free himself, to run from the visages, he fell deeper into the pit. He stood in the presence of hundreds of thousands of souls who'd been taken before him: despots and dictators, torturers, abusers and sadists; each of them suffering the same pain they'd inflicted on others. Harvey sensed and came to know pure and utter hatred, centuries upon centuries of torturous bigotry and enslavement, murder and rape; complete and wanton cruelty. He begged for forgiveness, pleaded to be set free, insisted on innocence and misunderstanding, and his cries for help were met with peals of unforgiving sinister laughter so loud he feared his eardrums would burst.

The further he ensnared Harvey, the more Jason's body shrank. A deafening weariness spread over him. He still heard the man's screams and pleas for help and understanding and mercy. It seemed with each new slice of evil Jason removed from the world the more he struggled to contain it. Even the longest-kept malevolence now burdened him in ways he never thought possible. He longed for rest.

After a final gaze upon the woman huddled in fear and pain, he mustered enough strength to leave. Shoulders slumped and his back bent, he walked out onto the street in search of a place to recover. He would have to entrust Nancy as Keeper until he could return. "It's getting so hard. Too hard."

Chapter 18

Nancy followed Jenna at a distance for almost two months; close enough to know her intent, yet far enough on the periphery to provide for a quick exit when needed to fulfill her main function. And Nancy's growing and emerging ability was needed. She chose her course of finding and keeping evil with great care. Two had to be taken when their belligerence wouldn't be tamed. Three others proved to be as frightened of that dark eternity as Marvin had been all those months before, and she released them. Though should the character of their intent darken, they would easily be found.

She saw Jenna thwart an attack by sliding into the victim and admired the swift takeover that removed the woman from harm's way. Jenna stayed inside her until she'd made it to the shelter and stepped away. The woman gawked around for a moment and then enrolled into their program.

Soon after receiving Jason's request to watch Jenna, Nancy became aware of a troublesome young man; a kid really. In his mid-teens, there was malice evident in his stride, a sneering challenge he projected to those who crossed his path. Now, his mean-spirited bearing would result in his own demise.

Nancy followed and watched as he leered at the girl, as she pranced through the aisles, and followed;

her short skirt and low-cut blouse mighty temptations to his raging hormones. With a fake southern drawl and easy smile, he lured her outside. She pushed him away when he pulled at and tore her top. He snagged her arm in a tight grip. "You can't get away with teasing this cock." After a few heavy-handed slaps to the face, he shoved her into a corner behind the concrete building and pushed himself against her. One hand pinned her arms above her head, the other hiked her skirt and thrust up between her legs. She screamed and fought against his more powerful body.

Nancy waited. Her inexperience prevented her knowing how he would die, she only knew he would. And she watched. And waited.

Jenna rushed through the delivery doors behind the store and missed her target. As Marvin had done, she ended up in the young man, but his strength and awareness proved too strong. The change in his facial features registered surprise at the invasion, but he renewed his efforts.

To Nancy's knowledge, up to that point Jenna never tried controlling a man, much less one who was intent on doing harm. Before, it had always been women she'd entered and took control of; women whose intent focused on self-preservation, rather than fighting, which made the effort easier. Jenna's voice echoed between the wings of the building in an oddly masculine register. "Diane, a little help here!"

Nancy moved forward and called out. "Jenna, don't. Not this time. Get out, get away from him."

The boy's awareness of Jenna slipping into his body allowed him to see what the living typically couldn't. He turned to face Nancy, and his grin exuded menaced delight. Though Jenna tried to respond, her own words didn't find a voice. "Ah, new meat." The actions Jenna tried to force upon him failed. The body twisted at the hips and the free hand groped lewdly at the flesh protruding from his open zipper. "Come on, bitch, come and get some of this."

"Diane, you come out here now," Nancy commanded, still keeping an eye on the struggle between Jenna and the boy. Diane burst through the wall of the building and Nancy pointed to the struggle.

Diane strode over, grabbed the dangling testicles and squeezed. A strange, unearthly howl burst from the boy's throat, and he lost his grip on his victim. The girl cowered to the pavement, her arms and hands covering her bared breasts. With his attention on his genitals, Jenna struggled to free herself. The blurred visage of hands brushed against a long, thin bump attached to the waistband at the kid's side. Jenna grasped it and swung at his midsection with all the force she could muster. The knife blade swiped through Diane and sank into the boy's diaphragm, tearing a long gash in a lung. Surprise splashed across his face and, in a gurgling gasp, his body doubled over. Jenna raised the arm and swung again. This time the knife sliced through his neck. He fell to the ground.

Jenna stumbled toward the side of the building, slid to the pavement, and sobbed. The boy lay bleeding out, gasping to fill his lungs. Diane stood hovering over the girl, who'd fainted into a heap in the corner.

"You," Nancy said, and pointed to Diane. "Get the girl into the store, and make her ask for help."

"How?" Diane's voice sounded small and weak.

"This is not the time to play coy. I've watched you

help her," Nancy said, nodding at Jenna. "Now, just do it."

Nancy waited until the girl lurched around the corner of the store and then turned her attention to Jenna. In a quiet voice she said, "Oh, Jenna. What have you done?"

"I didn't mean to. I just wanted to stop him. He's going to be okay, isn't he?"

Nancy ignored the question. "Do you know how serious this is? When Jason finds out…"

Jenna's tear-filled eyes pleaded for understanding. "I just—I wanted to, I was trying to get her away from him, that's all. That's all I wanted to do. I don't know what happened."

Nancy listened to the boy's breath rattle in his chest with a rasping gurgle and kept him in her gaze. "You better get out of here. Go home, Jenna." One last long, heaving inhale then exited his body in a slow whisper. "Quick."

Jenna rose and ran through the back wall into the storeroom of the building, back the way she came.

"Brandon, you come over here now," Nancy said to the boy as he rose from his body. She wondered if she'd be able to show him what fate might await and release him, or if would she need to take him and keep him, locked in misery for eternity. He turned to face her. His anger raged, but instead of resisting, fighting to stand in place like others did, he bellowed and rushed at her. Her body shifted and surrounded him. Nancy heard his taunts, his threats, for only a few minutes while she pushed his existence to the depths of darkness.

Chapter 19

Though Diane grated on Jenna's nerves early on, an honest friendship began to develop. She regretted leaving the woman behind and hoped the disastrous results wouldn't be enough to make Diane change her mind about helping again. But the tone of Nancy's command left serious doubt there could even be a next time.

The realization she caused someone's death rattled Jenna to the core. Her mind became a jumble of confusion. She longed for the security of Marvin's arms, but since Tommy had been in the world of the dead longer than anyone else she knew she wanted and needed his advice. She emerged from the storeroom and rushed toward home.

She wrestled with the decision during the short yet interminable elevator ride to the top floor. Should she head straight to Tommy and Mike? Or run to Marvin who would either offer comfort or begin to chastise her for again interfering with the living?

The elevator doors opened and noise coming from their own suite solved the dilemma for her. It sounded like a party was in full swing, and she headed down the deep-padded carpeted hallway. Not that any living soul would've heard her footsteps, or the laughter and boisterous conversation emanating through the door. She paused to gather the proper demeanor. Rolling and shrugging her shoulders to release the tension she feared would be evident, she brushed fingers through her hair and plastered a smile on her face. Stepping through the door she forced a false brightness into her voice when she asked, "What's the occasion?"

A line of people standing in front of the sofa turned to greet her.

"Well, it's about time," Marvin exclaimed, his smile meeting her as she strolled in.

"There she is!" Davy rushed to her. "Girl, do you know how long I've been looking for you?"

"Davy." Jenna accepted his air kisses. "Oh, well, here I am," she said as if she hadn't been purposely avoiding him since hearing of his return. The declaration sounded false even to her ears.

Mike raised a goblet in her direction. "You're way behind the rest of this drunken crew. Let me get you a glass. Red or white?"

"Dude, champagne first." Tommy waved the bottle. "I saved enough for her. Tonight is about her, after all."

"Me?" Jenna scowled at Tommy and made her way to Marvin's open arms. She gave him a peck on the cheek, and greeted Colleen and Patrick with swift hugs. In her distraction over the incident and the commotion of all the guests, she didn't see the man seated behind them and headed for the bedroom. "Just let me freshen up."

As she made her way back into the room, Tommy held a glass of champagne out for her. It took a split second for him to notice the shaking hand and the 'help me' expression on her face. "Here, let your Uncle Tommy set this on the coffee table until you recover from the surprise."

She smiled at Tommy to make sure he recognized the appreciation that registered in her eyes and let him lead her toward the couch. "I have a surprise? What is it?" Jenna asked with as much normalcy as possible.

Davy took her other arm. "There's someone here to meet you. It's a good thing he's a patient person and I've been able to find ways to entertain him around here for so long."

Gianni rose from the couch with arms outstretched. He grasped her hands and planted a kiss on the back of both, kissed both cheeks, and took a step back to admire her. Waving a hand in Davy's direction, he said, "*Bella*. Pay no attention to him. How perfect a meeting."

Jenna recognized the famed designer. She didn't need to be a fashion hound, as Diane and Davy both certainly appeared to be. The circus-like media coverage of his murder had been more than enough to familiarize even the most casual observer. "Mr. Versace, what a pleasant surprise."

Davy stood beaming from ear to ear. "He's agreed to do your dress."

"My dress? What dress?"

"For the wedding," Mike prompted.

A quick sigh escaped from Jenna, her shoulders dropped, and her eyes lowered in apology. "I never agreed, all I said was I'd think about it."

"Oh, but you must. The designs, they are all swirling around up here." Gianni rotated a finger at his temple. "Ever since Davy showed me your photograph. *Bella*, you shall be the most beautiful, the most stunning bride, you will make...Iman look like Quasimodo." The entire group laughed appreciatively at the joke. Gianni smiled for his audience, lifted Jenna's hand, spun her around as if in a dance, and continued to admire her. "Now that I see you in the flesh, may I say, something special emanates from you which utterly fascinates, an aura surrounds the auburn hair, a certain sparkle in the green eyes, the line of the chin as it sweeps to an elongated neck cry out for my touch. *Señorina*, the picture did not do you justice at all."

Marvin taunted his guest in good humor, "Hey, hey, careful there."

Davy leaned into him. "No worries, Marvin. He's one of us." Davy swept a gesture toward the group.

"I know that."

"No, silly, I mean he's gay."

Jenna laughed. "Well, Mr. Vers—"

"Gianni. You must drop the formalities. We are friends now."

"Gianni. Thank you, I'm sure you're exaggerating. But, I do feel bad that Davy made you come all this way before anything has been settled." Jenna turned her face to Davy and raised an eyebrow.

"Nonsense. Now, after we've finished celebrating your engagement—you are engaged, are you not—then we shall measure and I'll be off." He looked her over head to toe again. "I cannot wait to get started."

"But, what if my answer should be no?"

"No? You would say no to me? You would turn down a genuine Versace?" The incredulous sound of Gianni's voice increased with each question.

Tommy, who'd stayed silent all this time, piped up. "Oh, come on, Jenna. You know you want it. Really, I mean look at that face." He pointed to Davy who stood with longing. "How could you bring disappointment to that face?" Then Tommy added his own hang-dog puppy eyes and smile. "Or this one. Please."

"Or this one?" Marv added, moving toward her from across the room.

Marvin's gentle plea sent her into a tailspin. Now that she'd found a means of being useful in this life, Jenna stood torn between her need for independence, her drive to accomplish what she'd put her mind to, and her love for Marvin; between wanting to make him happy and keeping promises she'd made to herself during years of growing up being shuffled from family to family in the foster care system. Her expression of confusion and consternation served to cover up the more immediate issue. "Marv, it's not that I don't want to get married. Honest. But…" She fished for a reason and, after stammering, finally landed on something she figured would appeal to his sensible side. "Isn't it kind of wasteful to have a beautiful gown that will be worn only once? And then what will I do with it?"

Versace broke in to the conversation before Marvin got further than opening his mouth. "But, I must design for you. Such beauty as yours should be properly adorned. So, for you, I shall design a dress that will serve many purposes."

Jenna reached out with both hands to grasp Gianni's and she managed a slight smile. "Well, then, how can I refuse such an offer?"

"*Bellisima*!" The great fashion designer pulled her into a bear hug and kissed both cheeks.

The room broke into a cacophony of happy sounds as each deadhead pushed through to embrace her and shake hands with Marvin. The loudest voices belonged to Davy, whose waving hands augmented the beaming smile and "Oh, my God's," and Tommy, who blurted, "Far freaking out!"

Marvin let out a laugh, grabbed Tommy in a headlock, and scrubbed his knuckles across the back of his head. "Your sixties are showing again, hippie!"

"I know, isn't it great?" Tommy poked a finger through Marvin's stomach.

Mike, who always tried his best to get Tommy to ditch all the 60s' expressions, let it pass with no more than a brief scowl and broke open another bottle of champagne. The group gathered in a circle, Mike filled glasses, and then raised his own for a toast.

Diane breezed through the door, concern in her voice. "Jenna. Jenna, are you—" She stopped halfway across the room, stunned. "What the hell is this?"

Tommy broke away from the circle to intercept and greet Diane with a cheery, "Diane, come in and join us." Jenna saw him mouth in profile, "Not here," with a serious expression before he continued. "Mike, get Diane a glass so she can join the toast."

"What is this? Did I miss something somewhere along the line?" Diane allowed herself to be led toward the circle, consternation painted across her facial features until she recognized the guest of honor. She broke from Tommy's grasp, took the proffered glass of champagne from Mike without so much as a glance of thanks, and made a beeline to Gianni, the earlier episode evidently swept aside. "Gianni Versace? Why, Davy, I had no idea you had this kind of influence or I would've insisted on an introduction long ago." She held her hand out. "I'm Diane. It's a pleasure to make your acquaintance."

Gianni bowed graciously but with reserve, his lips grazing the back of her hand. "*Buona sera.*"

"How ever did Davy convince you to visit our common neck of the world?"

Gianni tipped his glass in Jenna's direction. "Why, for that vision of beauty, of course, how else?"

Before Diane could issue a withering response to match the furled brow, Davy beckoned to her and raised his glass high. "Diane, sweetie, come stand over here with me. There was about to be a toast to our guest."

Mike lifted his glass. "To the world's most famous designer."

"Well, most famous dead one, anyway," Marvin added.

"Now, Marvin, was that called for?" Colleen asked after she took the requisite sip.

"No, no, but he's quite right," Gianni said. "I dare say death certainly added to the acclaim."

The circle broke into small groups of animated conversation. Jenna approached Tommy and whispered, "I need to talk to you."

The two exited to the hallway where Jenna recounted what happened in as much detail as she remembered. Jenna worried the huddle may not have escaped the notice of Marvin; she imagined him stealing expectant glances at the door. But she knew Tommy, though a total goofball most of the time, could be entrusted to find solutions to the most troubling situations of the dead. She hoped he wouldn't fail this time.

Chapter 20

By two a.m., with Davy, Versace, and Diane ensconced in another room, everyone returned to their respective suites. Jenna stood on the balcony overlooking the city after asking Marvin for time to gather her thoughts. She tumbled the day's events over and over in her mind, and sipped on a glass of wine. It had been an accident, a pure accident. But how would she convince Nancy? Or this Jason who appeared to infuse such terror in the dead? According to Tommy that would be paramount to staying alive. It always unnerved her to hear the dead refer to this existence as living, and remembering his words sent a visible shiver through her.

Marvin came out, placed his jacket around her shoulders, and drew her close. "It'll be okay, kiddo."

Jenna turned into his chest and wept. "Oh, Marv, I wish."

He kissed the top of her head, then lifted her face with a finger under the chin and kissed her; a soft, gentle kiss. "Can you tell me what happened?"

She nestled into him and remained silent for a long time, gazing out at the miles of glittering lights. "You're going to hate me," she stated in a quiet voice, and told him the whole story. At the end she said, "I know I always accused you of being bullheaded, stubborn, and arrogant. Who's the arrogant one now?

Oh, God, Marv, I messed up. I really messed things up this time, didn't I?"

"Tommy'll figure something out." He led her inside, helped her undress, and tucked her into bed.

She tossed and turned for a long time, her mind swirling with different scenarios, different arguments, different punishments. Realizing she'd been disturbing him, she turned her back to Marvin, heaved a long sigh forcing her body to relax, and lay still.

****

At the other end of the hotel, leaning on a pillow propped against the headboard, Mike prodded all the information he could from Tommy, who paced the length of the bedroom. "There's got to be a solution to this."

"This isn't going to be easy Mike, she's been warned. More than once. I know she's trying to help these people, she's trying to save lives. But, I'm afraid. How many warnings did Marvin get before Jason came for him? I don't know. And it was only Nancy's intervention that saved his ass."

Mike realized that had been the last time he'd seen the goofy, fun-loving kid this serious and concerned. "A hot shower always seems to help you think."

"All I'm doing is thinking, dude. I can't shut it down. Man, don't we have any weed around here? I could use a good toke to settle my brain."

Mike shook his head. "Sorry. I'd think the wine and champagne would've helped."

"Dude, this is some heavy shit." Tommy stopped pacing and looked down at him. "I'm exhausted."

Mike knelt on the edge of the bed and patted the mattress. "Sit, a massage might help you relax, take

117

your mind off things."

Tommy rolled his head in circles against the kneading palms and drew his shoulders in a downward motion to help ease the knotted muscle. "I guess I have to trust that Nancy will understand. That feels good, thank you."

****

The next morning, Marvin peeked over at the sleeping Jenna, slipped out of bed, dressed and went down the hall. He called out as soon as his head was through the door to their suite. "Hey, Mike, Hippie. Wake up. Where are you two?"

Marvin stood in their kitchen when Mike emerged. "Brody, what the hell, man? It's six o'clock in the morning. What are you doing?"

"Making coffee. Jen's still asleep."

"Well, so were we." Mike plopped onto the couch. "You can be a total pain in the ass, do you know that?"

"Sorry. But, look, Mike, I know Tommy knows what happened. Jenna told me. He's got to help us figure this out. Hippie! Come on, wake up." Marvin held a cup under the amber flow with two more at the ready.

"Stop yelling. He'll be out in a minute. You know it takes him a few minutes to un-bale the cotton in his brain." Mike walked into the kitchen and took the full cup as Marvin swapped it out for an empty one.

"Well, I'm sorry if Jenna's life is—"

From experience, Mike knew the belligerence in his voice meant Marv was about to go off on a rant and smacked his shoulder. "Brody. Calm down. We know what happened, and we're here to help. Tommy was up half the night thinking about it. Just give him a few

118

minutes, would you?"

With his arms stretched above his head, Tommy walked out of the bedroom and let out a loud yawn. "Dude, are you happy now? You woke the dead."

Mike swiped the second cup of coffee from Marvin's grasp and walked it to Tommy. "Here. Sit. Clear the cobwebs. Marvin will wait." He looked over, dropping to the couch, his body language leaving no doubt. "Won't you, Brody."

"Yeah, yeah, fine. Whatever." Marv came to the living room and plopped into a chair.

Mike slung his feet up on the coffee table, next to Tommy, who'd tucked his feet up under himself. They sat in silence until Tommy tipped his head back to drain his cup. Mike took it from him, went to the kitchen to refill it, and then returned to his spot.

"Now?" Marvin asked upon seeing a range of expressions cross Tommy's face.

Mike turned to assess, but Tommy spoke up. "Okay, now, let's think about this. It was Nancy who was there when Jenna…well, when the accident happened, right?"

"That's what Jen said, yeah."

"So, where was Jason?"

"I don't know. Why are you asking me?" Marvin stood and headed to the kitchen. "I think we should just get the hell out of Dodge, is what I think."

"Dude, won't work. You can't run. He knows. I don't know how he knows, but trust me, he does. I mean, the minute you went for the poison that night in the diner, something truly lethal to kill Jenna, he showed up, right? And, so far with Jenna, we haven't seen any trace of him."

"So?"

"I'm just thinking out loud here. If things stay calm, she stays out of trouble…"

Mike waved his cup in the air. "Brody, bring the pot over."

"Here in the city? Good luck with that." Marvin heaved a sigh and mumbled, "Jesus H., I need a vacation."

Tommy planted his feet on the floor and sat up straight. "That's it. Dudes, I think that's it."

"What?" Marvin halted in his tracks.

"A vacation." Tommy stood and started to run for the door. "Isn't it time for the cruise?"

"What're you doing?" Mike called out as Tommy disappeared into the hotel hallway.

"I'll be right back." Tommy's muffled voice filtered through the closed door.

Marvin ran over and stuck his head out the door. "Where are you going?"

"To get Jenna!"

"Not naked, you're not! Get back here and get some pants on first. What're you, crazy?"

Tommy stopped and laughed. "Oh, sorry, dude, I forgot."

"You forgot," Marvin said sourly, and turned inward to Mike. "He forgot he didn't have pants on? How do you forget something like that? What is it with you two, anyway? Jesus H, every time I come over here—"

"Oh, can it Brody," Mike said. "And let him get through if you want him to get dressed."

Marvin moved into the room with the coffee pot still in his hand and Tommy walked through to the bedroom. Marvin leaned over to top off Mike's cup, and moaned, "Oh, for the love of God."

"Don't say it. I'm going, I'm going." Mike followed Tommy into the bedroom and left Marvin standing there shaking his head.

Marvin put the carafe back on the brewer and called out, "I'll get Jenna."

He walked to the other end of the hotel and called to her as he went through the door. She answered right away. "In here. Are they up?"

Marv followed the sound of her voice and found her in the kitchen, fully awake and dressed. "Yeah. Do you believe that schmuck? He was gonna run over here buck naked to haul you out of bed."

"Tommy?" Jenna asked, smiling.

"Do you know another schmuck?"

"I know another one, all right."

"Don't start with me," Marvin said, and pecked her on the cheek.

"Oh, don't worry. I think I've started enough." Jenna sipped at her coffee.

"How long have you been up?"

Jenna let loose a low sigh, moved to the small dinette to sit, and responded in a dull, tired voice. "I was awake when you got out of bed. So, what did he say? Does he have any ideas about what I should do?"

Marvin grabbed one of the cups they kept on the counter next to the brewer. "Well, I don't know what he has in mind, exactly, but—"

"So, what are we waiting for," Jenna asked, rising from her chair. Cup in hand, she headed out the door.

After he poured his coffee, Marvin followed her. He figured with her frayed nerves, any idea, any guess, no matter how elementary it sounded, to extract her from the trouble she was in would help calm her at least a little bit. Halfway down the corridor, Tommy and Jenna stood exchanging good morning hugs.

"Don't you worry, I'm gonna fix this or I'm not your Uncle Tommy."

The elevator chimed and they froze in place, each with their eyes wide and peeled on the doors. Jenna, who'd been holding her breath, sighed when a middle-aged couple emerged and headed down the hall in the opposite direction.

"I thought sure it would be Jason," Marv said.

"Something tells me he wouldn't need an elevator. Geez, I hope they aren't booked into any of our suites," Tommy said, watching the couple's progress until they stopped at a door and shoved the key card into the lock. "Nope. Okay."

"Thanks for thinking positive, Marv." Jenna shot the remark over her shoulder as they continued on.

"Come on, Jen. I'm just looking at it from my own experience," Marvin said as they moved through the door into Tommy and Mike's suite.

"Come on in, sit. Help yourselves." Mike gestured to the couch and indicated the carafe he'd placed on the table.

"What, no bagels?"

"Did you bring them, Brody," Mike asked.

"Hey, hey, you don't have to sound so churlish. I'm just trying to lighten the mood a little. It's been a rough five hours."

"Rough on who?" Jenna huffed, and turned her attention to Tommy.

He perched on the arm of the chair Mike sat in. "I

say we go on the cruise—just like we planned and promised last year."

"That's it? That's your big idea?" Marvin asked, leaning forward in his seat on the couch.

"What you're saying is, I just run for my life." Jenna's head dropped forward. She ran a hand across her forehead, and kneaded at the pounding of her temples.

Tommy responded to Jenna, "No. There's no running for your life. If Jason wants you, Jason takes you."

Jenna smiled. "Well, then I'm good, right? I mean, wouldn't he have been here by now?"

Shrugging, Tommy said, "Maybe. Who knows. Don't get me wrong, you didn't just interfere this time. You've committed the ultimate crime of the dead. There could still be dire consequences. But, I'd say the more time that passes without any incidents, the better things look for you."

Mike nudged his thigh. "What's keeping him, then? Marvin knows what could happen, he's seen it. Jason swooped in the instant Marvin went for—"

"Dude, no need for the gory details, okay? But, I think it's Nancy. She's managed to get some kind of influence." Tommy put on his best James Cagney mobster accent and finished with a laugh. "If it wasn't for her, see, Marvin here would be sleeping with the fishes, see?"

"Jesus H, hippie, does everything with you have to relate to a movie."

With a deep scowl at Marvin, Mike fired back, "I thought you wanted to lighten the mood, Brody."

"So, that's it then? We leave town?" Jenna asked to

get the plan back on track and glanced around at everyone for confirmation.

"Okay." Marvin stood ready to leave. "Not that we need to pack or anything, but…"

"Wait, what?" Jenna stood and tugged on his sleeve. "You may not have to pack, but I need things."

"It's nothing but a big sailboat. Believe me, you don't need anything."

"I don't care. *I'll* decide if I need anything." Jenna poked an index finger into his chest.

"Oh, brother, here we go. You always have to make a big deal out of things."

"Who's making a big deal? I'm just telling you I can make my own decisions."

"What decisions? I'm not making decisions, I'm trying to explain to you that you don't need to take anything." Exasperated, though he didn't know what caused the greater part of it, Jenna's situation, or Mike and Tommy, who'd come to enjoy the sparring and started to laugh, Marvin turned to them. "Would you two jokers explain this to her, please?"

"He's right, Jenna. All you take is you. You can't be weighed down by stuff," Mike told her.

"Besides, dude, there's nowhere to stash things without them being seen. And, I don't think you want to be causing any more trouble for a while—even the fun kind."

"Fine, then what are we waiting for, let's go," Jenna said with belligerence in her voice.

"We'll come get you once we've cleaned up around here. Wouldn't want to freak out the maids when they come in to scatter the dust around."

"I'll clean out the coffee stuff and get the trash if

you make the bed," Tommy offered to Mike.

"Deal," he replied turning to Marvin and Jenna. "See you in a few."

Jenna waved and walked out with Marvin close behind. He wasn't quite ready to give up the point. "There, you see how easy that is? Why can't you—"

"Come on, Marv, stop. I can't do this right now."

The defeat in her monotone voice sent a pang of guilt to the pit of Marvin's stomach. It was odd because even his mother had lost the ability to evoke guilt from him years ago. He caught up to Jenna, wrapped a protective arm around her, and kissed her on the cheek. Not sure he believed what he was about to say, but a deep gut instinct *noodged* at him, he gave in to provide the moral support she needed. "We'll go, we'll have fun, and you'll see…Tommy can lift anyone out of a funk. By the end of the week, everyone will have forgotten all about it."

Chapter 21

Nancy spent hours wandering the dark city, slipping through pools of streetlight, out of shadow and back again. Needing time to sort out the sequence of events, to think of a way to save Jenna, she did her best to ignore Jason's constant requests. In her mind, it would take quite an intricate debate to convince him that what Jenna had done was a good thing. Neither shadow nor light brought any answers.

In the early morning hours, as the sky began to lighten on the distant horizon, just like any other deadhead, Nancy had no choice but to respond to his command. A loud, stringent insistence that belied his drained state pummeled her brain. "Nancy, you come here now."

Compelled to turn and head toward him, she asked with wariness and fear evident in her voice, "What do you need?"

"You know what I need. There was an incident."

"Yes, but…"

Jason's voice softened. "You have no need to fear me. But, I will have an explanation."

Twenty minutes later Nancy found herself in Eastwood Metropark, northeast of the city that would soon be awakening to the hustle and bustle of the living. Amongst a small and secluded clearing, between railroad tracks and the Mad River, with trees beginning to spread their canopy of new leaves, she stood before Jason. "You look tired; thin."

Jason heaved a sigh. "I'll recover in time." He locked eyes with her. "It's not me you should be worried about."

"Please, Jason, I'm sorry. You don't need to—"

"If the deed warrants punishment, you will deal with it."

Nancy's gaze dropped to the dew-covered grass. "Yes."

"Now, tell me."

She had no reason to doubt he already knew everything, but Nancy did as requested and played through the event in as much detail as she could muster. "She was shaken; visibly shaken. And I sent her home."

"I allowed you to speak with her after the first incident, yet she has disobeyed. She interfered and now is responsible for taking a life." His voice grew stern. "This is the highest offense. Why have you allowed her to walk away after such a thing? Why should she escape penalty?"

"She didn't mean for it to happen. It truly was an accident. She became caught and, in her frightened struggle to free herself, panicked."

"But had she not interfered this boy would be—"

"Continuing on his path of destruction," Nancy pointed out.

Jason stared at her for a moment, and then nodded. "Perhaps. Yet, should one of us have decided the when and how of his death?"

"But that's just it. She didn't decide." Emboldened, despite the possibility of being chastised, or worse, Nancy continued, "What about the when and how of the future deaths he would have claimed? In doing this, Jenna has actually saved lives."

"What part of their lives and future is our business?"

Nancy found the key to her response in his question and barreled on. "Isn't that exactly what we do? Ensure the future? Ensure that those who are unrepentant in their evil can do no future harm? Jason, look at him. Look inside me and see him. He'd already taken lives, he would've killed that woman."

Jason's eyes bore deep into hers. Nancy became aware of what he heard, saw, and felt as if experiencing it herself. He heard the boy, this Brandon, roar with anger and saw a menacing grin spread across his face as he sensed the encroachment. A hand reached out, searching; not to escape but to pull Jason in, in an effort to inflict pain and calamity to another soul. Jason issued a long, low, hearty laugh with its own sense of cruelty. "You wouldn't want to know the things you would suffer, but shall I give you a taste of the thousands of years of the horror that inhabit me? Come, reach out. Touch me," he goaded. He locked a grip on the clawing hand and held it fast. The boy cowered in misery and tried to pull away. Jason's laugh grew loud, his deep bass reverberated through the clearing, and the branches of nearby trees shook as if they shivered in cold fright. When he felt the boy had seen enough, when the boy's deafening scream assaulted his ears, Jason loosed his grip and the boy retreated, mewling.

Nancy followed Jason's gaze as he lifted his face to a sky with a full, bright sun. A hawk floated on the updraft of breezes toward a bank of high, thin clouds that looked like wisps of feathers on wingtips. "You best take care with that one. Keep a firm grip," he said to Nancy.

She nodded acknowledgment. "Each evil creates more, doesn't it? Is there doubt about what the future would hold—our future—if he had lived? What if we could stop that from happening?"

"What do you propose?"

"Let me go find her. Talk to her again. She means well, I know she does."

"Many have meant well and ended causing much pain and suffering in others. You know this or I would not have chosen you. You would do well to remember that," Jason reminded her.

"I do and it's precisely why I want to help. I don't mean this to sound impertinent, but Jenna's intent is to stop these kinds of incidents, and I wonder what would happen if we allowed her to do so."

Jason responded without need to consider. "No. It cannot be allowed."

"Look at yourself, Jason," Nancy stated quietly. "You've grown so weary that it's taken you weeks to recover. It would save you, save all of us, every Keeper who exists… It would extend our ability."

Jason sat on the ground and leaned against a maple tree to think. A long while later, he roused himself to answer her, and found Nancy walking around the clearing. "Why does this effort mean so much to you?"

She jumped a bit at the sudden sound of his voice and went to sit with him. "To save people from pain and suffering, especially the type that Jenna tries to halt…. I thought you knew this about me. I thought it may have been why you chose me, because it's what gave me my strength." When Jason made no remark, she continued, "I had a sister, older by six years but we were close. She wasn't too bright when it came to relationships; boyfriend after boyfriend committed affront after affront. It wasn't until one of them attacked me that she woke up. Her grief and anger at my loss fuel her behavior. She was good once, but what she does to men now is wrong. What if we were able to stop people like her from hurting others?"

"By interfering with the living."

"By somehow breaking up the altercation," Nancy insisted. "Which is all Jenna wanted and tried to do."

Jason went silent again and Nancy stayed as still as she could.

"You will go find her and bring her to me."

"Jason, please. Consider what I'm proposing."

"You will bring her to me," he stated, then stood and returned to his recuperation among the cool, quiet stillness of the trees.

Chapter 22

"Though your trip sounds—" Gianni placed fingertips to his lips and sent a kiss out to the universe "—wonderful, *Bella*, I shall see you soon." He planted kisses on both of Jenna's cheeks and parted ways with the group at his own departure gate to head to Paris for fabric, then on to Milan where he would begin work in earnest on her promised gown.

Everyone else hopped the earliest flight headed to Miami they could find listed on the departures board. With no first class cabin available, Mike had to make due with traveling like "a regular schmuck," as Marvin put it to him. With the world's economy in shambles, they didn't need to fight over seats; most were empty, unless you counted all the deadheads, then it could've been considered a full flight.

As happened the year before, several deadheads recognized Tommy from Epstein's Deli. Soon after take-off, Tommy leaned into the row where Marvin, Jenna, and Davy sat. "Dudes, can I get you anything? Snacks, beverage?"

A man in the next row back said, "No, no. You sit and relax, Tommy. Anything you or your friends want, you let us know. We'll take care of it."

The exchange impressed the hell out of both Davy and Diane. Leaning over to Davy, she said, "Wow. That's some reception. It's like everyone knows who

Tommy is."

"I know. Maybe we should go to brunch some Sunday. I hear he does a pretty fabulous job at the grill."

The group's every wish for snacks, or drinks, was granted, but after a while even Davy groused that Diane took undue advantage.

In Miami, Tommy and Marvin both yelled "Dibs" on the first taxi headed to the cruise ship port. Not able to fit everyone into the same cab, the group was forced to split up. Along with their respective other halves, Tommy and Marvin melded their way in among the people actually paying for the ride.

Tommy stood on the front seat pushing his head and torso through the roof, and joked to the disgruntled Diane standing on the sidewalk, "Hey, there's always the hood or trunk."

She fixed Tommy with a withering stare. "Squeezing into someone's luggage, while it may get me there, is not my idea of a vacation. But thanks for the offer."

Davy nudged her. "Oh, honey, you need to relax and lighten up, or it's going to be a long week."

Diane pursed her lips. "What I need is decent transportation. If you'll show a little patience, I'll find us one."

Two deadhead kids, who looked to be barely out of high school, exchanged a glance. One broke into a big smile and said, "What the hell, bro. It'll be just like car-surfing, only this time it ain't gonna kill us!" The other laughed and they hopped onto the hood of the taxi, face-forward, latching their fingers around the hood at the windshield behind them.

Marvin and Jenna crawled into the crowded rear seat with an older couple and their fidgeting grandson who kept thumping a shaking leg through one of Marvin's. "Jesus H, give this kid some valium or something," he said to the couple, who didn't respond, of course.

Up front with Mike, Tommy insisted on riding shotgun. His usual antics caused the driver to break out in a sweat. The man pulled a crucifix and chain around his neck from under his shirt. Making the sign of the cross, complete with a touch to the lips, he mumbled, "*Santa Maria. Mi Dio.*"

Tommy switched on the wipers for more fun.

"Ow, what the hell?" The boys on the hood each yanked a hand into the air. "Hey! What're you doing? Turn those things off, man."

"Sorry, dudes. My bad," Tommy called out, flipping the switch to the off position.

At the docks, the two boys jumped off and beat a path toward the Disney liner while Jenna, Marv, Tommy and Mike stood waiting for their straggling companions at the curbside drop-off. Almost half an hour later, Davy emerged from the back seat of a shining, gray stretch limousine and helped a smiling Diane out, though her smile was more of a smirk. "Looks like you should've waited."

"No biggie." Tommy's smile beamed. "I enjoyed my ride."

"Now, which one of these behemoths is ours?" Mike asked.

"Heck if I know, dude. Guess we have to check the departure board," Tommy replied, and headed down the sidewalk toward a crowd of people (dead as well as alive) staring up at a bank of signs.

They all stood studying the dock information. After noting a name and departure, Diane turned her gaze to the ships, and then back to the departure board. "That one," she said finally, pointing to a ship with a streaming school of brightly colored blue and purple fish painted along the side.

"Whatever. Suits me." Marvin linked arms with Jenna and started walking.

The gang gathered on board and Diane, of course, insisted on haunting a suite. Since Mike had the first class experience the year before, he agreed with Tommy they could just hang out on the deck in a couple of chaise lounges. Marvin and Jenna headed for one of the bars to snatch a glass of wine they could take to the bow.

In port at Nassau, Davy regaled everyone with the tale of his dreary experience. Left to his own devices and unable to help himself, he wandered the ship assessing the couture, more often than not shaking his head in disgust at the loud Hawaiian shirts straining to cover the paunches riding over the plaid Bermuda shorts of the men. Wishing instead for men in Speedos, he found the sight of women hanging around the pool in barely-there string bikinis a bit distasteful. He wandered off and ended up perched on a stool to watch Diane flirt with every trim, well-dressed male deadhead she laid eyes on.

Diane stood on the dock and glared at the three-mast schooner with a sour expression. "You're kidding, right? It's a joke?"

"Nope. This is it. Absolute heaven on sea." Tommy sighed.

"But, there're no real staterooms. Where am I supposed to stay?"

"Granted, the staterooms are small, but how much time are you going to spend there? No, no, no, these babies," Mike said, pointing to the ship. "These are made for a true sailing experience: out on the deck with the spray of the water on your face and the salt breezes blowing through your hair."

Diane scowled. "Well, have fun, kids. I'm staying here at a hotel where I can get the kind of service I deserve."

"And exactly who do you think is going to serve you, your highness?" Marvin asked. He raised the volume as she walked away and said, "You know what, you need to learn to live a little. Davy, what about you? Going or staying?"

Davy didn't make up his mind until Tommy badgered him. "Dude, I'm telling you, this trip is like, wow, man, far *out*. The party spread they put out on the island, to die for."

Aboard the ship they stood in a small group at the bow waiting to set sail. The jostling for position to avoid people bumping through them got to be too much for Marvin. He made his way to the makeshift bar at the stern and helped himself to a margarita. The bartender did a double-take at the sound of something crunching against glass and rubbed at his eyes when a circle pattern showed in the dish of salt.

"I wondered if you'd remember," a familiar voice said.

Marvin turned to find Dennis, and Connie with a new person in tow, headed in his direction and raised his glass. "Of course we remembered," he lied, not wanting to give away the real reason they'd made the trip. During introductions, handshakes, and hugs Marvin whispered into Dennis' ear, "What happened to what's-her-name?"

"Mel? They broke up. Guess relationships aren't any more stable here than in life," came the whispered answer before Dennis stood back, his brows raised in hope, and asked, "Mike and Tommy?"

"Of course. And Jenna," Marvin announced.

"Wasn't she the fiancée you were so gloomy about last year?" Connie pushed her hand into a cooler, brought up two beers and handed one to her partner, Carla.

"The very one," Marvin replied, his face beaming.

Carla accepted the beer and offered her thanks, then turned to Marvin. "So, how did you get a message to her to come, or was it just a coincidence?"

"No, no, she's with us now."

"Oh, my, God! You actually went through with it? You killed her?" Dennis asked.

"If he'd done that, he wouldn't be standing here right now." Nancy's voice came from behind Marvin.

His face lost all color (if that was possible), his grin disappeared, and he turned to greet her as she moved into the circle of friends for hugs. "Nancy! What are—I mean, I'm glad you made it. Last year's gang wouldn't be complete without you."

"And it's been added to," she responded, indicating the bow of the ship with her head. "Why haven't you introduced them to Jenna and Davy?"

"Oh, we just hadn't gotten that far," Connie said. "But, I'm sure we'll love her."

"Who's Davy?"

"I do believe he's right up your alley, Dennis," Marvin blurted out, and immediately wished he could take it back when he realized the double entendre. "I mean, oh, screw it. You know what I mean."

Dennis laughed. "That's what I like about you Marv, always straight and to the point."

"Well, you got the 'straight' part right," Jenna joked, sliding into the group at Marvin's left. "I'd have to question the rest of that statement,"

"Hey, hey, watch it there, kiddo. You could be cruising for one." Marvin winked and balled up a fist, doing his best to put on a carefree front for Nancy's benefit.

"These must be all your friends from last year. I'm Jenna." She held out her hand to Carla who stood sandwiched between Dennis and Connie. It wasn't until she'd made the full circle that she noticed Nancy, standing to Marvin's right. Her spine stiffened and the gasp of surprise didn't go unnoticed.

"Jenna, I'm so glad you're here with us this year." Nancy nodded at her. "It's going to be a great week."

While the conversation continued around him Marvin studied Nancy looking for signs of deception in facial expression or body language; anything to indicate trouble might be in store.

"Do we have a full boat this year?" Connie asked, dodging an oncoming body heading for the bar. "I mean, besides these annoying tourists who keep walking through us."

"I haven't seen anyone I don't know, yet. So, what, with you..." Nancy pointed to Jenna. "And Davy, that makes nine this year, right?"

"Don't forget me," Diane accused, pressing her

way through a crowd of the living. "Do introduce me to your friends, Marvin."

Marvin made introductions all around. Of course, when he got to Dennis, Diane's demeanor changed in an instant. She crossed to him with an appreciative expression on her face even as she checked him from head to toe. "It's such a pleasure to meet you."

Despite his concern over Nancy's presence, Marvin broke out in a genuine laugh. "Oh, this is going to be a very entertaining week."

Chapter 23

Marvin voiced his complaint only once at seeing Tommy, Mike, and Dennis run around the ship naked. "Jesus H, do you have to?"

"Oh, leave them alone, Marv," Jenna chastised. "Who cares?"

"Yeah, dude, who cares?" Tommy chided from his perch in a hammock strung between the rails at the bow. "Besides, I seem to recall you streaking down the beach and going all Woodstock at some point last year, too."

"And, honey," Davy said with a grin on his face. "Some of us rather enjoy the view."

Restful fun and light conversations brought the whole group together each day. They raided the galley of left-over food for midnight snacks at the bow of the schooner and told stories of how they'd messed with the living—hiding and moving things, putting them back in their proper place after the owner had thrown arms up in frustration. Tommy even badgered Marvin into recounting his escapade of trying to kill Jenna at Mr. C's restaurant which had resulted in a newspaper story claiming the place was haunted. By the time Marvin finished the tale he had everyone in stitches, even those who had heard the story before. They gathered at the bow to watch dolphins play in the waves of the ship, or lie in the sun, and the days slipped by.

Nancy bided her time, looking for the just the right moment to approach Jenna. The situation was serious, more serious than her inquiry with Marvin the year before. He'd been so full of love and longing, at that point anyway, that his threats to kill were only wishes on candles. The situation with Jenna had become tenuous. As much as her intentions were in the right place, as Jason had so pointedly spelled out, Jenna's actions had gone terribly wrong. Nancy considered that, perhaps, the day of the island beach party might afford her the chance she needed.

The crests of the ocean waves sparkled in the afternoon sun sending playful reflections across the canvas sails when something brought a stampede of living feet trampling through the small circle of women sprawled out on the deck to soak up the warmth.

"Watch out, ladies." Mike laughed. "You could end up with a foot somewhere it doesn't belong."

Jenna and Diane scrambled to port, and Connie, Nancy, and Carla scooted starboard, all uttering profanities.

"This has been the most tedious trip, I can't imagine what the hell they all find to be so exciting that they have to run like a herd of heifers," Diane grumbled.

"You might want to try joining in once in a while to relieve your boredom," Dennis quipped. "And spare us poor common folk the pain of listening to you gripe."

"Now, now, children, be nice to one another." Tommy sat upright in the hammock, placed a hand to his brow and peered out to the horizon. "It's the island. Far out, dudes. You know, tomorrow is going to be absolutely groovy."

"Hey, hippie, your sixties are showing again," Marvin called out over his shoulder.

"Oh, come on, dude. Don't bum me out when it's time to ball, man."

Jenna looked over at Tommy and grinned. "Time to ball? Excuse me?"

"You know, party, have fun," he explained. "What did you think I… Oh, you thought it meant sex. No, that meaning hi-jacked the word sometime in the seventies or eighties. Sorry."

"Whatever. Jesus H., could you stick to the present for us youngsters?" Marvin asked, making everyone laugh. Tommy, though dead the longest, really was the youngest of the bunch.

Nancy smiled but trepidation at the inevitable task held sway over her emotions. After the party the next day, the schooner would make a nighttime-leg sail back to Nassau. And she still hadn't figured out exactly how to break the news to Jenna.

The sun lowered in its famous Caribbean flash of green and, with no artificial light for leagues upon leagues, stars cast pinpoint reflections off the peaks of the waves on the water and the moon cast a glow to lay a beckoning path to the sand. As the ship eased into the bay on the leeward side of the island, Tommy rose from the hammock and kicked off his sandals. With no place to stow his clothes, he slipped them on.

"Where're you going?" Mike asked.

Gripping the edge of the schooner's side rail with his toes, Tommy poised for a dive into the ocean. "Dude, I don't know about anyone else, but I'm ready to hit the beach."

A small pile of assorted shoes appeared at the very point of the bow. The water parted eight more times in tiny splashes as the few forward passengers pointed and wondered aloud what kind of fish could be jumping.

Nancy recognized her opening and perked up. She pushed her way through a growing crowd of the living, ignoring their murmurs about a momentary chilled breeze coming in off the water, and dove in.

Their clothes dripped as the deadheads walked up onto the beach. Everyone started peeling off wet clothes while Tommy bumped out bars of the classic stripper music. "Bah-bah-dah-dah, bah-bah-da dah." Everyone chuckled but Marvin.

As Tommy hit the cymbals, Jenna pushed down at the waistband of her jeans. Marvin's scowl deepened. "Whoa, whoa, whoa. What are you doing?"

"Let her be, Marvin." Nancy tossed her blouse over some low-lying foliage next to soggy apparel.

Mike slapped Marvin on the shoulder. "Lighten up, Brody. Just because you're a prude doesn't mean the rest of us have to be."

"Come on, Marv. Don't be ridiculous. You'll dry faster if you take these off," Jenna said as she grabbed the bottom hem of his polo shirt to lift it over his head. She tossed the shirt over a rock and reached out to unbutton his pants.

"Don't do that."

"Come on, Marv, don't be silly. Nobody here cares."

"Besides, dude, we've all seen what you got."

"She hasn't." Marvin pointed to Diane and, pointing to Davy, added, "Neither has he."

Diane rolled her eyes and tossed a droll response in

Marvin's direction. "Oh please. Like I'd be interested in what you have."

A slight breeze wafted down from the crest of the small island causing a noticeable shiver to run down his torso. "See," Nancy observed. "Listen to her Marvin. Jenna knows what she's talking about."

"Fine. Far be it from me..." Marvin turned away from the crowd and unbuttoned and dropped his jeans to the sand, then kicked them up with a foot and caught them. He laid them on a large rock along with his polo shirt.

Davy appeared too enamored of the island to even respond to any of it. Slack-jawed and eyes wide, he gawked around in awe, as his expression altered. He peered up at the groupings of palms, the other trees and shrubbery, gazing from one end of the small crest to the other, and took note of the clear areas. "How big is this thing?"

"Come on, I'll give you a tour," Dennis offered with a beckoning wave.

The two headed off along the beach. Exchanging a shrug, Mike and Tommy followed. The powder-soft sand parted under their feet leaving four sets of barely-noticeable prints.

Nancy's stomach did a few somersaults but she forged ahead. "Let's go for a walk," she said to Jenna and Diane. "You two should see the view from the center up there."

"Well, that leaves the three of us to man the watch," Connie joked. "Marv, how about you take the first stretch while Carla and I wander around?"

"Whatever," Marvin said, snuggling down face first into the still warm sand.

Nancy read his thoughts as easily as she had a year ago. He was well aware that she had been part of the group last year and included in the plans for this repeat, but questions nagged at the back of his mind. He couldn't shake the gnawing at the pit of his stomach that there was more to her last minute appearance than joining the group for another cruise. *Oh, Jesus H, stop it already,* he told himself to fight off the urge to follow and eavesdrop. Despite the heat enveloping him he shivered at his next thought. *You're beginning to sound like your mother.*

Nancy sent words to him no one else heard. "And that wouldn't sit well with Jenna. You know that, don't you?" Then she turned to Jenna and Diane, and pointed to the top of the isle. "Come on girls, let's leave him to wallow in his self-pity."

Chapter 24

Jenna didn't know exactly what her punishment would be, but Marvin's distinct shudder when she had asked him to recount his experience was enough to tell her it might be gruesome. She and Diane stood side by side under the copse of trees, silent and trembling, and waited for Nancy to speak.

Nancy looked out over the glistening water to gather her thoughts as well as to steel her resolve. If Jenna tried to escape, there would be no choice but to take her to Jason by force. Being caged with the boy she'd killed would be a horrendous experience and Nancy hoped she could avoid needing to do that. "You have to be made to understand that what you've done cannot be tolerated. It has to be talked about."

"You know I didn't mean for it to happen."

"But it did. How many times were you told not to interfere with the living? Yet you not only kept at it, you practiced, and you plotted."

"To help those people. To save them from pain, not to cause it."

Turning her eyes on Diane, Nancy said, "And you... I know you weren't given the same warnings but you've been on this plane of existence, in this world long enough to know this kind of thing is not allowed. I'm sure Jason will agree with my decision to let you off the hook."

The tenseness in Diane's shoulders eased, but concern for a newfound friend replaced her usual haughtiness. "And Jenna? You can't mean—"

"It's not up to me." Nancy let out a soft sigh. "I wish it was because, believe me, I understand what you're trying to do. But Jason is not so lenient."

"Don't I even get credit for saving some lives? All that counts with him is that one man died, is that it?" Jenna's voice found strength and grew from its previous whisper. "It was unintentional and he knows it."

"He's old, Jenna. Very, very old. He's been the head of our Council on this continent for eons and he will not be easily swayed."

"There's got to be a way to make him understand," Diane interjected.

Jenna's shoulders lifted and her back straightened. "What you're saying is that he's too old to change with the times. Then he shouldn't be in the—"

"I'd be mighty careful if I were you," Nancy warned. "That's a dangerous attitude to adopt. You have no idea what he's capable of, the power contained in that body or that mind."

Jenna ratcheted her attitude down a notch. "I just meant that he needs to listen to reason."

"No you didn't. You meant exactly what you said, and it was disrespectful. Now, you listen to me, both of you. I'm trying to help you here. So, stop fighting. All it can do is cause more damage."

Jenna's voice contained apology but retained an underlying desperation. "I'm sorry, but there has to be a way to convince him."

"Jenna, let her talk."

With hands together placed against her lips, almost

in a position of prayer, Nancy dropped her gaze to the sandy loam for a minute. Her voice was quiet, blending with the night breeze that floated off the water. "There are millions, men and children included, who suffer at the hands of others. The people who commit atrocities against their own... Well, it's our job, the job of Keepers, to reign them in. But, we do it only in death. We know about them, the cruelty they harbor inside, and we keep watch over them. We're there when they cross over, ready to take them. Just like you didn't have a choice but to obey when I issued my orders behind that store, they can't avoid the fate they've earned." Nancy paused to let the knowledge sink in. "You know I've been charged with watching you, Jenna. I've had plenty of time to think about what you're trying to do, and I understand it. I know there's no malice behind your intent, either of you, and I hope that makes a difference. But, ultimately, it's up to Jason. When we get back, my orders are to take you to him."

"Both of us?" Diane's voice rose incredulous.

"No, just Jenna." Nancy nodded at her. "Jenna, I'm sorry."

Tears welled in Jenna's eyes. She turned and ran.

"Wait," Nancy called out. "Jenna, come back."

Marvin heard her sobs before she hit the expanse of beach where he'd buried himself. Forgetting his nakedness, he rose up out of his warm cocoon of sand, caught her in his arms, and rocked her, stroking her hair. He saw Nancy running down the slight slope and raised a hand to stop her from intruding. Then, keeping an arm wrapped around Jenna's shoulders, he led her away.

Diane came to Nancy's side and they stared after

the two figures as they walked along the beach toward the southern tip of the island.

"How awful will it be," Diane asked after Marvin and Jenna were out of earshot.

Nancy shook her head. "I don't know."

Diane drew in a breath and held it for a moment. "As much as I hated to admit it, even though it may get me in trouble, my opinion of Jenna rose substantially with each victim she managed to help. This hits me right in the gut: I want to help. Isn't there anything we can do?"

"We'll see. I have something rattling around in my head. If we play it right, maybe…"

****

The tour of the island took a long time. Davy ooh-d and aah-ed with each new view, and more than once he uttered a quiet "Hush, I'm thinking," when Mike, Dennis, or Tommy questioned what he was up to. With arms folded across his chest and a hand held to his chin in thought, every so often he mumbled, "That could work…"

When they hit the windward beach, Tommy yelled, "Last one in wears combat boots," and ran into the water. Mike and Dennis followed, leaving Davy standing under a small group of palm trees staring up toward the center of the spit of land. He walked to his left, stopped to study the view, returned to the trees, walked to the right to appraise the angle, and again returned to the deepening shade to study some more.

"It's going to be the most gorgeous wedding the world has ever witnessed," he said to himself. Then he turned to find three heads bobbing in the ocean. He called out to them, "Guys! This is it, it's perfect."

"Well, look who finally woke up," Mike said.

"Dude, come on in." Tommy issued a wave of welcome. "There's nothing like skinny-dipping to relax the mind."

Already as naked as the rest, Davy waded out to them. By the time he stood with them, he had to be on his toes to keep his head above water. He grabbed Dennis around the waist to keep from drifting with the current. "Move in a little closer so I can touch bottom."

Dennis carried him toward shore and set him down. "Better?"

"Much. Now, look. Right up there," Davy swept a hand upward. "What do you think?"

After they all stared for a minute, Mike said, "Uh, okay. So what?"

"So what? It's perfect." Davy beamed with pride.

"Perfect for what, dude?"

"Marvin and Jenna's wedding, of course."

A smile slowly spread across Tommy's face. "Describe it."

Davy laid out his plans for the entire event in intricate detail; where each thing would take place, the reception, the way the whole island would be lit up for a ceremony at dusk. When he finished, Dennis whistled long and low. "Wow. It sounds spectacular. You wouldn't need an assistant, would you?"

"Maybe." Davy turned to assess the man as well as the offer. "Sure, why not?" Jenna had been pretty glum the entire trip and, thinking his ideas might cheer her up, he made his way out of the water. "Dennis, if you're going to assist me, let's go.

Following Davy's lead, Dennis swiped as much ocean from his body with his hands as he could, and asked, "Where to?"

"To get the bride's approval, of course." Davy's excitement mounted but he kept it under control. There was no flapping or waving of the hands, he was all business as he strode down to the beach where they'd landed and found Nancy, Diane, Connie and Carla sitting on the sand, huddled in a circle. "Where's the bride and groom? I've got some excellent ideas…"

Nancy looked up at him. "This is probably not a good time right now, Davy."

"Why? What happened?"

"Sit. I'll explain."

Nancy went through the story once again, and finished with, "I think what she's doing is a good thing, but Jason isn't convinced."

"Obviously I do, too, or I wouldn't have been helping her," Diane interjected. "Not that he ever took a swing at me, but that bastard husband of mine could use a lesson or two."

"But even if we manage to talk Jason into letting her go, he can't make autonomous decisions. He may head it up, but he still answers to the North American Council and, ultimately, to the World Council."

Davy squirmed a bit. "Well, that could blow a big hole in the wedding plans, couldn't it?"

Carla stopped drawing mindless circles in the sand. "Connie and I are willing to help. What can we do?"

****

They had all dressed and regrouped on the beachhead by the time the morning sun glowed pink on the horizon. At one point or another through the night, everyone had tried to engage Jenna in conversation. She responded with one-word answers or silent shrugs.

Now, they all sat in a row on the sand. A dinghy, loaded with supplies for the day's festivities, dropped from the side of the schooner and the crew rowed toward shore.

"Will they go back for passengers?" Jenna asked.

"They'll be back and forth, they've got a lot to bring over," Mike replied, squinting into the sliver of light that had risen directly in front of them. "Why?"

"I don't feel much like partying now. I think I'll go spend the day on board."

"Dude, what gives?" Tommy nudged an elbow into a silent Jenna. "Anything I can help with, you just say the word."

She replied in a quiet voice, "I'm okay. Really." Then she wandered away to sit on some rocks, her feet washed by waves.

Mike leaned in to Marvin, who had been more morose than usual, and whispered, "Is it bad, Brody?"

Marvin nodded. "I think so."

"What can we do to help?"

"I don't know, you'll have to ask her," Marvin snarled, and jutted his chin toward Nancy.

The forward crew member jumped from the dinghy, gripped the bow, and pulled the nose to the sand. The other two handed off crates and chests that were stacked far enough up the beach to avoid the water, though there would be no need to worry about a high tide; there was no such thing in the Caribbean.

All eyes were on Jenna—dead ones anyway—who sat staring out to sea. With the first load done, the crew pushed into the water and began rowing back to the ship for the next load.

Nancy moved and sat between Marvin and

Tommy. "I have an idea, if she'd only listen to me. She seems to trust you, would you talk to her, Tommy?"

****

While the rest of the group rummaged through the trunks left behind looking for items to pilfer for breakfast, Tommy went and settled on the rock next to Jenna. The two sat silent for a long time. Then he found the words to encourage her to open up. "Come on, tell your Uncle Tommy all about it."

"Marvin's so disappointed in me."

"No, he isn't. What makes you say that?"

"Well, wouldn't you be? I mean, look at him, sitting over there, shoulders slumped like he's been defeated."

Tommy stole a glance at Marvin. "No, I think he's worried about you."

"I let him down. We're finally together again, and I let him down. That's the worst part about this whole thing." Tears dripped down Jenna's cheeks and she swiped at them with her forearms. "Tommy, I didn't mean to hurt that kid."

"I know."

"Well, that doesn't seem to make any difference. I don't understand. Nancy said her cult, or whatever she belongs to, works to keep bad things from happening and that's all I was trying to do; stop bad people from hurting good people."

"She'd really like to talk to you."

"I don't know what more I can say. She has her orders and, according to Marvin, it'll be a lot less scary if I go without being forced."

"I sure don't have the experience he has on that score." Tommy lifted his eyes skyward. "Thank God, and he's probably right. But, it seems like Nancy's on your side. She's a good person, Jenna. I mean, look what she did to help Marvin. She talked Jason out of taking him, or doing whatever it is he does. She says she's got an idea, I think you should hear her out."

Jenna stood, waded into the clear shallow water, and chased a small fish with her toe. After it wriggled away to hide in the shade of a rock, she tilted her head to one side and asked, "Will you go with me?"

"You know I will. Now, come over here and let your Uncle Tommy give you a hug." He held his arms wide and she buried her head in his chest.

Chapter 25

Dennis picked up a plate he'd left on the buffet table for a second to grab a hunk of roasted pork. A young woman shook her head to clear it. "What the—I swear there was a full plate of food right there a minute ago."

"Where?"

She pointed to a corner of the buffet table. "There. But it just disappeared. Didn't you see it?"

"I didn't see anything."

"The sun must be getting to me already." She wiped her brow with a damp napkin, dug a hat from the bag hanging on her arm and tugged it into place.

Throughout the day, living passengers spotted the occasional odd occurrence; empty bottles and cans dropped into waste bins as if falling from the clouds (though they could have been thrown by another passenger when nobody was paying attention), rings of pineapple and chunks of papaya vanished from the plate of fruit, handfuls of shrimp and chunks of lobster blinked out of sight. Other than those innocuous incidents, the group of deadheads avoided the living, preferring to have a quiet day. Until a game of beach volleyball broke out; guys against the girls.

The deadheads gathered on the sidelines to watch and enjoyed the shenanigans the women used to distract the men. Bikini tops' straps slipped, every so often one of the women would bend down to provide a good glimpse of cleavage, or spend a little too long bending over, buttocks in the air, to retrieve an out-of-bounds ball. None of it seemed to be working; the men still overpowered them. But even Jenna managed a slight smile at the tactics.

Nancy noticed the subtle change and, thinking to distract Jenna from her problems, nudged her with an elbow. "I think maybe the girls could use a little assistance. What do you think, should we go help?"

Jenna turned away and made no comment.

"Well, I'm in." Tommy stood and made his way to the middle of the formation. "Come on, girls," he said to the team, who didn't respond, "it's time to get serious and kick some ass!"

Connie, Carla, Diane, and Nancy joined him, each shadowing one of the live women.

"It's looking a little lopsided there. Should we go join the men?" Marvin asked.

Mike laughed. "Brody, do you have a death wish? The guys are gonna get creamed, big time."

"We'll see about that." Marvin went and stood in the middle of the men's team.

It was ladies' serve. A girl tossed the ball into the air and powered it over the net. The return came back fast and hard. Connie slid her arm into the closest player and the ball slammed over the net. "Holy crap, Suzie," said one of her teammates. "Where the hell did that come from?"

Suzie rubbed at the strange tingling in her arm and laughed. "I don't know, but I really nailed it, didn't I?"

The game volleyed back and forth for almost five minutes, and all Marvin managed to do, really, was get in the way. His body got bumped through with elbows and knees, and even a couple of head butts before Jenna called out, "A lot of help you are. You might as well be on the women's team."

"You could help, you know!"

Jenna stood and said, "Okay, you asked for it. I might as well enjoy what time I have left." She jumped into the midst of the ladies with a grin on her face, and assisted a return.

"Hey, hey, hey. What is that?" Marvin asked, ducking away from the ball as it whizzed past. "Traitor!"

"Ah, go step in front of a bus," Jenna taunted him, and laughed for the first time in a week.

Marv winked. "Go fall down a flight of stairs!"

The deadheads roared approval prompting Dennis and Davy to join up with the women.

Mike stepped in to help Marvin. "We are definitely outnumbered, Brody. You do realize we're going to lose, right?"

"I do," Marv replied, then leaned in to Mike. "And as long as it puts a smile back on her face, it'll be worth it."

More than a few times during the game, the ball suddenly altered course and fired back over the net to the men's team. "What? Wait a minute, how is that possible, you weren't even near the ball. That should've gone out of bounds," one complained.

"It's a secret weapon, boys," Tommy responded. "Face it, you guys are done for."

"Ya'll are cheatin'," a man's southern drawl accused as he ran to retrieve the ball from the water's edge before the ocean grabbed it.

"Oh, now, honey, don't be such a spoil-sport," Davy chastised. "It's not very attractive, you know, no matter how hunky you look in that bathing suit. Especially from a kindly southern gentleman like yourself," he added in his best Alabama dialect.

The game had gotten so competitive, a crowd of passengers gathered to watch the fun, and the sideline cheering sections chose sides. The skipper stood at the net and waved his hat through the air. "Twenty all. There's a round of drinks and a platter full of shrimp for the winning team when we get back on board."

"For the match point," declared Suzie, poised to serve.

Even as her cohorts cheered her on, a man waved his teammates closer to the net. "Move up for the lob, that's all she's got in her. We'll take possession and go for the win."

"You know, I don't think I like his attitude," Diane said, sliding fully into the woman's body. She added a power to the serve that sent the ball flying low across the net, right between two of the men. They both lunged at it and missed. The force of it slammed right through Marvin's midsection and ditched into the sand with a thud.

Marvin wrapped his arms around his stomach. "Holy mother of Mary!"

A loud cheer rose from the female contingent with high-fives and hugs as they made their way to the canopied tables.

"God, I am suddenly famished," Jenna said, hugging Marvin.

"Well, then, let's go get you something to eat. And snag a couple of beers while we're at it, how's that sound?"

"Like heaven." Jenna slipped her hand into his and they made their way to the tables.

The rest of the group followed, helped themselves to platefuls of food and sat on the sand slightly removed from the living. Tommy put his plate down behind a rock and walked over to the coolers. "Anyone else need something to drink?"

He took orders, reached in and tossed them over one by one. The minute a can left his grasp it winked into the sight of the living. As it was caught, it disappeared. Tommy stood in place and kept an eye on a group of fellow passengers until he saw one glancing his way and lobbed the last can across the distance.

A scream let loose and the woman jumped and ran. "Oh, my God, did you see that? Did you see that?"

Tommy placed a hand to his mouth with a sly grin. "Oops."

Another one jumped up, her eyes darting around. "What's wrong, what happened?"

"Over there, a can of something just, just..."

By the time everyone's attention went from gawking at the frightened woman to the place she pointed with a shaking hand, there was nothing left to see.

"Randi, sweetie," a man said, sidling up to her. "I think you've had a little too much sun."

"Or rum," someone suggested and loud laughter rolled out to sea.

Chapter 26

While the crew broke down and packed up for the final leg of the cruise, the deadheads moved to the west side of the spit of land, along with all the paying passengers, to take in the performance of the sunset. The tips of waves sparkled in the final rays that broke through wisps of pink-hued clouds and trade winds rustled hair.

Nancy found herself in a quandary again. She wanted to broach her idea with Jenna, yet she didn't want to kill the buzz the group displayed. If she tried now, here on the island, it gave Jenna too many places to run to avoid the discussion. The confines of the ship might offer fewer spots to hide, but the outcome could still be the same. Yet, she was running out of time.

"It's so beautiful here. Why can't we just stay forever, Marv?" Jenna asked, leaning her head on his shoulder.

"It would be nice, wouldn't it?"

Jenna bit down on her lower lip. "It would keep me from having to face Jason. I'm scared, Marvin. I keep wondering what's going to happen, what will he do?" Before he could respond, Jenna let out a soft sigh. "I'm sorry, Marv. I really screwed up, and I'm sorry."

Marvin placed a hand over hers. "It'll be okay, kiddo. You'll see,"

Scooting a few feet across the sand, Nancy put

herself directly in Jenna's sightlines. "I can't tell you what his decision will be, but I can tell you this much. I'll be there, and I'm going to be in your corner."

"I know you believe me, but—"

"No, I don't just believe you, I believe *in* you. I'll fight for you. I'll fight with all I've got. And everyone else here agrees with me, and wants to help." She waved her hands along the line of deadheads.

They fell silent as the sun's flash dipped below the horizon, and moments later the blast of a horn signaled the crew was ready to ferry passengers back to the ship.

Tommy stood. "We better go if we don't want to be swimming to catch up like we did last year. That was a hoot, but I think we've had enough fun at their expense," he said, nodding at the retreating group.

Everyone but Jenna and Marvin rose and headed back to the beach. Nancy stopped several yards away, turned to them, and waited. Though she could've commanded her to obey, preferring to keep it calm and friendly, Nancy called out, "You coming?"

Marvin rose and held out a hand for Jenna to grasp. She took it and stood with a desultory expression, and walked beside him with listless movements. When they reached her, Nancy spread her arms and embraced Jenna in a comforting hug. "We're all here to help, you have to trust in that."

"What can they do? What can anyone do?"

Nancy pushed Jenna to arm's length and met her gaze. "As odd as this seems, I think what you were trying to do is good. While I can't make any promises, I've got a plan."

Chapter 27

After an hour or so of instruction from Nancy, Marvin and the guys sat huddled at the bow of the ship during the entire final leg of the cruise and avoided the living as much as possible. Jenna and the girls disappeared for short bursts of time. Every so often one of them would return to the group, staggering and appearing light-headed, as if they'd downed too many shots of rum at the open bar. Tommy's brow furled in concern. When one rejoined the huddle at the bow bearing a smirk of satisfaction, the corners of his lips would turn up.

Everyone stayed quiet on the flight back to Dayton and for most of the ride to the hotel, as if lost in their own worlds.

When the bus ran past Epstein's, Tommy hollered out to the group. "Is anyone else as hungry as I am? Let's hit the Deli. My treat."

Marvin laughed. "Your treat. You're mighty generous when it's not costing you a thing."

"Dude, it's a figurative treat, right? Besides, are you gonna pass up a free corned beef and pastrami sandwich?"

"Not on your life!" Marvin grabbed Jenna's hand, and they leapt from the bus to the sidewalk.

Davy turned to Diane, who sat in the seat across the aisle. "I guess we're going to sample the fare sooner

161

than we thought." He pulled Dennis, seated beside him, to his feet and pointed to the side of the bus. "Come on, rumor has it Tommy's the best cook this side of a tombstone."

"Wait." Diane grabbed at the back of Davy's shirt to try to stop him. "I do not jump from a moving vehicle." She tugged on the cord to signal the driver to stop. He glanced up at the rearview mirror, but the bus never slowed. Diane pulled and didn't let go until the bus came to a halt. The driver yanked the emergency brake, and stomped his way toward the back to see what had snagged the line. He'd gotten more than halfway along the length of the vehicle when she released it, walked through him to the front and out the doors.

A cold shiver ran down his body as he threw his hands in the air. "It figures. These old rattletraps should've been retired long ago. Who pays the price? Me." His mumbling continued while the rest of the deadheads stepped through the side of the bus chuckling and he made his way back to the driver's seat.

After gathering on the sidewalk, they followed Tommy the block-and-a-half to the restaurant where they melded through the wall in a swarm. The place was empty, unless you counted the handful of deadheads. Colleen and Patrick were still lingering over coffee and a *kugel*, and rose to greet them. Through all the hubbub of introductions, Tina-I'll-Be-Your-Server-Today stood oblivious at the wait station filling salt and pepper shakers.

Once the vacationers had responded to all the usual post-travel questions, Tommy said, "We're a little early. We might have to wait until Moe and Tina clear out before I fire things up again."

"Wow, where is everyone? Is the place usually this empty?" Dennis asked.

"That'll be the day," Marvin retorted, moving into his typical booth next to the window. "Most days it's tough to find a place to sit and if you're not careful you could end up with someone in your lap. But it's near closing. The usual customers have already left for the synagogue."

"Grab a seat everyone. I'll go see what the timetable is." Tommy motioned for Mike to follow, went behind the counter and whispered something to him.

Mike disappeared through the back, then a moment later his face pushed through the wall. "Moe's in the kitchen hovering over a sink of hot water, scrubbing his spatula. I'll be back." He disappeared again.

Davy stood next to the drink fountain, an empty glass in his hand. "Hey, Marvin, is it okay if I help myself to a soda?"

"I don't see why not."

Davy shoved his hand through the top of the ice bin. Then he pushed the glass against the tab for his drink. The machine swooshed as the mixture flowed into the glass.

Tina's eyes darted toward the sound. Soda poured from the machine but disappeared as if evaporating in midair. The huge canister of pepper almost slipped from her grasp. A second later, with grit teeth, she swept her gaze across the empty tables. "All right. Fine. Here," she said with false gaiety, "let me start a fresh pot of coffee for you, too. How about that?" She stomped over to the brewer, slamming things as she went, and yelled toward the back, "Moe, I swear he's here again."

Moe, whose hearing was excellent even at what some would call his advanced age, ambled out and cocked an ear. Colleen took a sip at her coffee and ice rattled along the inside of Davy's glass as he shook a few pieces of ice into his mouth after draining it of soda. "More than just him, I'd say," Moe told her, and strolled into the back again.

Tina walked behind the counter, and angrily twisted knobs as she moved from appliance to appliance. "You want me to turn the grill and fryer back on for you, too, Tommy?"

The deadheads had been chuckling at her antics, but mouths dropped in awe when she uttered his name. "Uh-oh, I think she's on to you," Dixon, one of the regulars, called out.

Tommy collided through her as she went to gather her purse from the office. "I thought something was up. I think Moe's been aware of me for years. He must've told her because she hasn't been her jittery self the last couple weeks. Well, there goes *that* fun."

"The place is all yours." Tina marched through the diner, stopped with the door pushed open, slung her purse over her shoulder, and turned around. "But, let me tell you something," she said, shaking a finger at no one. "This place better sparkle when I get back on Monday morning!"

"Ooo, watch out, she might come after you with a cleaver," Dixon snickered as the door swung closed and Tommy started to take orders.

"My, we can get rattled by the mysteries of life,

can't we?" Colleen asked. "Why, you should've heard the maid this last week."

Sitting down across the table from her, Jenna asked, "Did something happen?"

"Well, dear, now I know I've said 'things are just things,' but this was my tea service. She'd taken my tea service," Colleen replied with an attitude in her voice that wasn't like her at all. "This was on this Sunday past. I did my best to avoid the woman, but when she started up with that vacuum I simply had to leave, it jangled my nerves so."

"I can attest to that," Patrick interjected.

"When I returned, I went to make a nice soothing cup of tea and everything was gone. Can you imagine? We searched every cupboard in the place, didn't we, Patrick?"

"We did," he agreed, and took a sip of his coffee.

"Did you find it? Did you get it back?"

"We did. Patrick found it in the room behind the registration desk. There it was, on a shelf, "dibbs" and the woman's name printed on a piece of paper taped to it," Colleen huffed out, and pursed her lips. "But, then on Thursday, we were sitting at the table with our tea, watching the afternoon news, and in she comes as pretty as you please."

By this time, everyone in the diner was held in rapt attention. "Oh, no," Connie uttered from the adjacent table. "What did she say?"

"She gave no heed whatsoever to the TV, stalked to the table and picked up the tray—tea pot, sugar and cream bowls, and all—and started to walk out. Thank goodness Patrick was on his toes because I was too flabbergasted for words. And, mind you, I don't rattle easily, do I dear?" she asked her husband.

"That you don't."

"What did you do, follow her down and take it back?" Dixon asked.

"Did better than that," Patrick gloated. "I snatched it right out of her hands."

Jenna gasped. "Oh, you didn't."

"I did."

The room broke into a round of applause. Diane raised her glass in salute. "Good for you. There's no reason to have to take that kind of crap from them, not after a lifetime of it."

"What did she do when it disappeared right out of her grasp?"

"She broke loose with a scream like you've never heard, and a string of words that would give a sailor cauliflower ears."

Patrick stood and took a bow through a second round of applause accompanied by hoots and whistles.

"Plates up," Tommy yelled from the grill, and began placing orders on the counter.

Mike reappeared from the back reaches of the restaurant and dropped a large rectangular box next to the cash register. He picked up two plates. "Burger and slaw; pastrami on Kaiser with potato salad?"

"Over here," came a response, and Mike dropped the plates in front of them.

"Come on, Brody, don't just sit there," he scolded, heading back to the counter. "Okay, I got two corned beef on rye with knish."

"Here, those are ours." Marvin took the plates, dropped them on the table of their booth and returned to help. "You're on your own for drinks this time," he called out to the room.

Between Marvin, Jenna, Mike, and Dennis, the food got served and the place became deadly quiet for the next fifteen minutes as food disappeared, even from their ghostly vision. Table by table, conversations started again as they leaned back in their chairs to offer compliments to their host and chef. Drinks were refreshed. If any living soul had passed by and bothered to glance through the window, it would've looked like some emergency had caused the diner to be suddenly abandoned. Dishes, cups and glasses, rumpled napkins and haphazardly scattered silverware littered the tables; chairs sat at odd angles and distances from tables as the deadheads enjoyed their evening of social reverie.

All talk ceased when Moe appeared from the back, a bag in one hand, and peered around the small dining room, his hand hovered to turn off the lights. Instead he went to the front door, turned in, and said, "Make sure you clean the place really good. I got a gut feeling there's an inspection coming up." Then he lifted the bag. "Oh, thanks for the sandwich, Tommy. Tina couldn't fry an egg without burning it, so I figure it had to be you." He left, locking the door behind him.

"Yep, he's onto you all right. But, it seems he's not bothered at all."

"Or scared. Huh."

"Dudes, there's no reason for him to be bothered or scared."

Mike and Tommy snuck over behind the counter, opened the box, placed thirty candles into the cake, and lit them. Tommy gave a nod to Davy, who stood poised at a bank of switches, and the place became doused in darkness, except for the glow that lit Tommy's face as he walked from behind the counter. He started singing Happy Birthday, and walked toward Marvin as the rest of the crowd joined in.

Moe stopped when the lights went out and, looking through a window, watched the glimmer of light float across the diner, and smiled. "Happy birthday to whoever." He walked away.

Marvin's face lit up in a grin. "Are you kidding me?" He rose from his booth seat and waited for the cake to be placed on the table. "Come here, you schmuck." He grabbed Tommy into a bear hug amidst the round of applause and scrubbed the back of his head with a fistful of knuckles. "Hippie, you are somethin' else, you know that?"

Tommy pulled away, laughing. "Dude, what have I told you about the coif?"

"Happy birthday, Brody."

"Mike, I don't know what to say. You two have been… I don't know how I would've…" Marvin hugged him. "Thank you"

"You're welcome. Now blow out the candles before they melt all over the cake." Mike spun him around and pushed.

Marvin blew out the candles. As he righted himself an expression of fear came over him, and he pointed to the figure standing across the street just a second before the diner lights flicked on. "Tell me I'm imagining things." When he and Tommy turned to Jenna, they knew he hadn't imagined it.

Save Nancy, Jenna must have heard what the others hadn't: Jason's command, a command no lesser deadhead could disobey. She tried to speak, but couldn't form words. She swallowed hard, her brow wrinkled, and then the smile on her face flat-lined. In a panic, Marvin and Tommy both whirled around to find Nancy. She, too, sat stone still, a grimace frozen in place.

"Marvin, no! Don't touch her," Tommy said when Marvin reached out for Jenna.

Worried, Colleen rushed toward Jenna, the daughter she'd never had. "What is it? What's wrong, dear?"

Mike put his arms around Colleen before she made it to Jenna. "There's been an, well, an incident."

"My heavens." Colleen clasped her hands to her breasts. "What kind of—"

Without uttering a sound, Jenna stood and walked through the glass window as Nancy went through the door. The crowd inside stood silent, squeezing together into a clump, their arms, legs, and torsos blended together, and watched as the two crossed the street and stopped in the pool of a streetlamp directly in front of the towering Jason.

"What's happening," a voice asked.

"Whatever it is, it doesn't look good," came a response.

Taking Colleen by the arm, Tommy moved back into the center of the diner. "Do you think you could organize cleaning up in here?"

"If it'll help, why of course." Looking toward Jenna's retreating figure, Colleen couldn't keep the concern from her voice. "But, is she going to be okay?"

Tommy looked out at the three figures who started to walk down the street. "I don't know. I hope so, Colleen," he said quietly. Then he addressed his friends. "Okay, you guys." The entire crowd turned to him, forcing him change tactics. "Colleen needs you to stay and help her clean this place up. Cruise people, just like we were taught on the way home. Let's go."

Chapter 28

"You disobeyed. You of all people would dare?" Jason's eyes bore into Nancy with an intensity Jenna had never witnessed in the living or the dead.

Nancy held her ground. "No. You didn't give me time. I would've brought her as soon as the party ended. I didn't want to hurt or disappoint those who love her." Nancy gave a jut of her chin toward Jenna, who stood silent, eyes cast down at the sidewalk. "I didn't want to frighten them or cause them undue pain."

Jason studied his protégé for a long moment. "I've told you, I will have an explanation. Now go." He pointed toward the southeast and followed his two charges down the street.

Once again in the park, Jason stood in the clearing between the train tracks and the river. In the ever-darkening sky, a bank of clouds rumbled and a colony of bats breezed overhead chasing insects in a series of acrobatics. Their beating wings and high-pitched squeaks drowned out the low, soft sounds of the flowing water. He held a hand out for silence before Nancy could utter a word, and studied Jenna.

At first her eyes fluttered as she tried to avoid his deep, penetrating gaze, but her strength was no match. His eyes shone with the intelligence of eons and she could not pull away. A dull ache filled her, painful yet not, like a weight pressing down; breath that wouldn't come. Her limbs grew heavy and useless.

"We have few rules here on this plane of existence. You have broken the most sacred there is. Even the living do not tolerate or condone what you've done. You've ignored the warnings; defied us." Jason pointed to Nancy. "It's only due to her intercession that you've been allowed to remain free. I will know why you insist on interfering."

"I've already expla—" Nancy began.

"I will hear it from her," Jason said, his voice flat and words deliberate. "For once, she will speak for herself."

Jenna didn't know how, but sound floated from her throat. "To help those people who are too timid and afraid to help themselves because they've been beaten down, either by words or fists. They deserve someone to stand in their corner."

"You killed a man, a young boy."

"It was an accident. You have to know that."

Jason nodded. "I don't hear or see regret."

"I was trying to move into the girl's body, to get her out of harm's way. I stumbled into him and got caught. His thoughts frightened me, and I panicked."

"I repeat: I don't hear remorse."

"You want me to apologize for his death, to feel bad about it, and I can't do that. I'm sorry if that angers you. He would've raped that girl. And killed her; left her exposed and dead in that back alley behind the store. And then he would've found another victim. Maybe not that same day, or the next. Maybe not for weeks or months, but he would do it again. And again. And again."

"You think you know this how? By some imagined

otherworldly sense you believe you've gained here?"

"No. Because I've seen it. I watched it. So many victims: women, children, even boys and men. I tried to help and was powerless in so many instances. Words and warnings had no effect then. Even hiding them couldn't save some of them. Now I have the ability to do something and you want me to ignore it."

"What good can come of it, of your interference? What can I expect if it's allowed to continue? More death?"

"People like him need to be stopped," Jenna insisted.

"By their own kind, not by us. We do not interfere with the living." Jason's voice boomed and she cowered.

"But we do. Plenty." Tommy stepped from behind a clump of wild elderberry bushes, just beginning to show signs of their tiny dark purple berries. "Sorry," he said to Nancy.

Jason chuckled in spite of the situation with Jenna. "I wondered how long it would take for one of you to step forward." He raised his volume. "The rest of you come out here."

He waited while the seven remaining deadheads stepped into the clearing forming a protective cluster around Jenna and Nancy. "What did you hope to accomplish by hiding? Did you think I didn't know you were there? I've been at this longer than... Well, never mind that. You say we interfere, Tommy. Yes, but it's nothing more than common trickery, for our own amusement, and no harm comes of it."

Nancy found her opportunity to speak on Jenna's behalf. "If we can interfere for the sake of fun, why not interfere for the sake of helping someone to safety, of saving a life?"

"That's what they were doing. That's all we wanted to do," Mike said. "Save a life."

Jason turned his gaze on Mike. "You've all been doing this."

"No," Diane spoke up. "Only Jenna and I."

"So far," Jason replied, studying the others. "I can see that."

Marvin's knees wobbled when he walked forward. "You remarked to me once that I was fading, getting dark around the edges, because of the things I tried to do." He turned his head toward Jenna. "If she was up to no good, if her intention is to do harm, wouldn't it be happening to her?"

Jason considered the presented arguments for a moment. "If this were allowed, how can I be sure none of you will...panic, I believe is the word you used, Jenna, when things go wrong again? How can I trust you? What reassurance can you give?"

"They've been practicing," Tommy blurted, then gawked around. "Uh, that was okay to admit, right?"

Jason raised an eyebrow. "It has taken many years for me to learn what you believe you are capable of. I don't doubt your ability to grasp lessons, they will come with time and effort, as mine did. But, I wonder if you have the strength..."

****

Jason's eyes captured them and his stature grew. Faces froze in fear, their bodies stiffened, and, his power absolute, he held them all for several moments. One by one he instructed the men to turn and leave. Then he dug into the minds of the women.

"There are things beyond your framework of understanding. Can you withstand the horror, even the nominal amount Nancy does at this time? Can you discern lies from truth, repel despair and agony, shed it as easily as rain might run down a back? Will you be able to refute false pleas of ignorance? Most important, will you be capable of not becoming that which you now wish to stop? It will be required if this activity is to continue. We shall see."

Though he kept a close, protective grasp on them, each woman faced what he kept buried within him; even his own protégé whose most recent take could be no match for what he held at bay. He exposed them to the despots of wars and serial murderers, allowed clawing waves of wanton cruelty and evil, dark enough to blot out the brightest sun, to touch their minds and hearts. Save for one, they recoiled. Yet none screamed; never pleaded to be saved or released.

It was Diane who surprised him. Certain of what he knew of her, Jason expected her to be the most delicate given her attitude of expected entitlement to leisure and finery, yet she proved to be the strongest of the five. She had laughed as if walking through some carnival funhouse. It pleased him, yet gave him pause. Those who found amusement in pain and suffering could easily be capable of imposing it. He penetrated deeper into her mind, searched for any sense of joy she may have experienced upon inflicting pain. He discovered a sense of triumph when she'd stopped men in their tracks, but found no enjoyment of the act. If pleasure in witnessing suffering was there, she had managed to hide it from him; a feat never accomplished by any.

Jason's imposing figure dwindled until he once

again resembled the old, harmless man so many deadheads witnessed shuffling along streets. One who sometimes appeared to be mumbling to himself. The only visible sign of power remained in his bright, piercing eyes. The group before him stood silent.

One more issue stood out for Jason as he silently contemplated how things had changed over the millennia. There could be no doubt he'd ensnared some whose infractions couldn't compare to the larger horrors inflicted by the evil he also held at bay. Jason looked inward and could see how the blackness crept and overtook all, became stronger, and increased the rate of his weakening state. It was the reason he'd allowed the experiment with Marvin. After his long silence, Jason turned his gaze to Jenna. "And how shall we police this…police force of yours?" he asked her, sweeping a hand around the circle of friends.

Everyone waited while Jenna searched for an answer. When Nancy attempted to supply one, Jason stopped her. "No matter what I may think, two Councils must consider this issue. If you can't answer me, how will you be ready to address their concerns?"

"When?" Nancy asked.

"I will call the first to convene in a week, on the lake island within the borders of Canada. You know the one."

Nancy acknowledged with a nod.

"Then go and prepare."

Chapter 29

Marvin stopped pacing and peered out the window of Mike and Tommy's hotel suite. "Holy Mother of Mary! Come on. It's been over a week already. How much longer is this going to take?"

"Now you know how I felt, dude," Tommy replied from his spot on the couch. "Jason and Nancy had you at the deli for four days last year, man. Four days. I was extremely bummed out, you know?"

Mike dropped the book he'd been reading into his lap. "Brody, you're just going to have to trust them. Jason let you go; you came out of it okay."

"Dammit." Marvin threw a punch through the plate glass to release his pent up frustration. He lost his balance and toppled, teetering on the edge of falling. He righted himself and caught a glimpse of five figures approaching the parking lot. "Hey, Mike, look down there, is it them?"

"Where?" Tommy, who'd moved faster, scanned the lot below. "Dude, I think so." He stuck his head out the window and hollered. Five hands waved through the air. On his way toward the bedroom, he tapped Mike's leg with a toe. "Come on, Mike, get dressed, we're going out."

"Why?"

"This calls for a celebration. I'm gonna fix the best meal any of you have ever tasted."

"Not so fast, hippie," Marvin said. "After Jason finished with me, I was exhausted."

By the time the two pulled on their clothes, they found Marvin standing at the elevators, his eyes fixated on the up arrow above the doors. After several minutes, it still hadn't lit up. Impatient, Marvin stuck his face through the metal panels. The top of the car rammed past his head. A bit dazed, he found himself face to face with the surprised expressions of the girls.

"Good lord, Marvin, was that really necessary?" Jenna pushed against his chest to get him out of their way.

"Well, excuse me for being anxious after nine days."

Jenna breezed past him. "Oh, quit your exaggerating."

"Don't tell me I'm exaggerating. You've been gone over a week," Marvin argued, and followed her.

"You know, you're worse than an old woman, Marv."

"Can it you two," Mike said. "I want to hear what went down."

"Yeah, what happened? I mean, obviously everything's okay because you're here, but—"

Everyone began talking at once. Marvin and Jenna argued, Connie and Carla questioned the actual time frame. In an attempt to answer them, Nancy hollered, "If you'd just give me a minute." Tommy and Mike repeated questions to anyone who would listen. Drawn by the commotion, Dennis and Davy came out of their room, adding to the uproar, followed by Colleen and Patrick rushing to inquire about Jenna's welfare.

Diane's face curled into a deep scowl and she

raised her hands. "Stop! My God, are you people always like this?"

Jenna turned on her. "Like what?"

"So excitable, jabbering over the top of one another. Calm down already."

"Hey, listen here, princess." Marvin poked a finger in Diane's shoulder.

"Okay, everyone stop right there." Nancy's voice rose above the din and the noise ceased. "First, yes, it's been nine days. Time isn't the same when... Well, it's just not. Everyone's fine." She scanned the faces of the four women who'd been so severely tested. "Tired, maybe, but fine. We're all in one piece. But, it's not over."

Marvin broke the stunned silence. "What do you mean it's not over?"

****

After a celebration at Epstein's, everyone returned to their suites for the night. Marvin and Jenna sat on the balcony, glasses of their favorite merlot in hand from a large stash he'd brought over during her absence in a rare moment of positive thinking, staring out over the city. "I'm not sure I understand this. Explain it again," Marvin asked.

"We have to go with Nancy to some conclave. Diane and I can't let her go by herself, it wouldn't be right. She can't be left to defend our actions."

"But I thought you said you all had to go."

"We do."

"Why, Jen? Why can't you stay here and let the others go?"

Jenna let out a soft sigh, and sipped her wine to stall while she formulated an answer, besides the obvious one. "Because we're all in it together, we promised to stick by one another. It'll be fine, Marvin."

"Nancy mentioned preparing for it. What does that mean?"

"We need to figure out how to convince this…council Jason heads up that what we're doing—I mean, what Diane and I have done, isn't terrible."

Marvin turned and grabbed her arm. "Wait a sec. That was a slip of your tongue if I've ever heard one."

"I don't know what you're talking about, Marvin." Jenna pulled her arm away and switched her glass to that hand.

"Bullshit! Come on, kiddo, come clean with me. For once, come clean."

"I'm telling you, there's nothing to admit."

Marvin stood and moved into her line of vision. "Jen, hon, this isn't sparring for fun. There's more to it than you're letting on." He forced her to meet his gaze. "Oh, my God. You're going to keep doing it, aren't you? And the rest of them—Connie, Diane, Carla, even Nancy—they're all in on it now, aren't they?" Jenna dropped her eyes to the parking lot below. "What, the five of you are forming some kind of vigilante gang?"

"Marv… No, it's not like that."

"Then what?"

"Look, first of all, I know you weren't aware of the hours I spent at the shelter before I moved in with you, because I stopped when we got engaged. I just…I don't know, it seemed fruitless. But you should know by now I can't stand around and let anyone get attacked like that if I can do something to stop it. And now I can. Now I'm capable. If they'll let me."

"And this council, or whatever, decides?"

"Yeah."

Marvin sat in his chair again and took small sips of wine until he drained the glass. No deadhead could ignore an order from Jason. If it indeed was an order, she had to go, she knew he understood that. The thing she didn't need to do was keep trying to save the world, but he also knew her well enough to not argue about it. It would be wasting his breath, he understood that, too.

Marvin sat in his chair again and took small sips of wine until he drained the glass, then rose from his chair to get a refill and stopped at the door. "When?"

"A week from tonight," Jenna responded softly, and Marvin went inside leaving her to sit, wondering why she felt so guilty for trying to do something good. When he didn't return, she went in to find him sitting on the bed, shoulders slumped, elbows propped on his knees and chin in his hands. She sat on the bed next to him. "Marv, I'm sorry."

"Are you?"

"Come on, don't be like that."

"Like what? I can't worry about you, now?"

She laid a hand on his thigh. "I'll be fine. You'll see."

"If you'd seen what I have, you wouldn't be so confident. If he changes his mind, you'll wish…."

Jenna didn't know if she could tell him she had seen it. Being allowed to tell him wasn't the question. She knew it wouldn't get her into trouble, especially since he had first-hand experience. But the visage hadn't affected her in the same way and she worried that might shatter his self-image. She slipped her arm around him and pulled him down to the bed.

Marvin snuggled into her and pulled her arm

tighter around his torso as if he needed the comfort of familiarity. "I suppose this means no wedding."

She picked up on his playfulness and replied in a quiet voice. "Will you forget about the stupid wedding."

"Oh, you'd like that, wouldn't you?"

Jenna smiled and nudged the small of his back. "Why don't you go step in front of a bus."

Marvin tugged on her arm. "Go fall down a flight of stairs."

Chapter 30

In the intervening days, the five women gathered in various places to discuss and plan. They ceased using one of the hotel suites because Marvin kept breaking in to express one worry or another, and when Davy interrupted to inquire about some detail for the wedding, Jenna snapped, "I don't care. Go ask Marvin, whatever he decides is fine."

"I'll take that as a definite yes," Marvin hollered from their living room. But when Davy came to him with the question, Marvin wasn't smiling. "Why are you even bothering with all of this?" He poked a thumb in the direction of the circle of women out on the balcony. "If they can't convince this council to agree, they may not even be allowed to come back."

"They'll be back," Davy responded with the wave of his hand. "Have some faith, Marvin."

"Dude, this is turning out to be some shindig," Tommy said. "And what I'd like to know is how you're going to manage to get everything out to the middle of the Caribbean Ocean."

"I've got elves." Davy grinned. "No, seriously, you know as well as I do, Tommy, some of the living are quite capable of sensing those of us on this plane, even hearing and talking with us. Word has spread and people all over the world—alive and dead, by the by— are already working on this to make it happen."

The statement caught Mike's attention. He turned off the television and asked, "How are they hiding the expenses?"

Davy responded with a sly smile. "It's amazing how little attention billionaires pay to the balances of their offshore accounts, or the exact whereabouts of the ships they don't even know they own, or their yachts and planes when they aren't using them."

****

Whenever Nancy needed to leave to complete her duties as Keeper, the other girls spread out across the city to practice entering various women to control their movements and then step back to observe the effects; the importance of unawareness tantamount. If the living remembered, it could lead to problems.

Three days into the training, Connie faced a different situation. This time it was the real thing. She returned to her friends, her face haggard and drawn. "I think we need to expand our practice to include men. Taking over a man's body is tougher than I imagined."

Nancy jumped from her seat on the balcony where they once again gathered, thinking the group had done fairly well. "Why, what happened?"

"Well, he didn't fight back against his attacker. But he was so pissed and scared, it was like it overwhelmed his thought patterns to where I barely managed to wrest control over his body and get him the hell out of there."

So the practice continued but focused on sliding into men. And they again took to coming together to compare notes anywhere but the hotel. At the end of each day, they met the guys in the deli.

"We'll need to leave tomorrow," Nancy announced between bites of her sandwich, and the mood suddenly turned sullen.

"I still think we should go with you," Marvin said.

"We've already had this discussion. You'll stay here and wait."

Though Nancy's inflection left no room for argument, Marvin needed to try. "But—"

Jenna scowled. "No. No buts, Marv. Nancy knows what she's talking about. Having you guys along might anger the members of the council. What if they thought we were trying to pull something over on them?"

"Yeah, like that could happen." Marvin paused, a French fry in mid-air on the way to his mouth. "We couldn't hide ourselves from Jason, how could we possibly hide our presence from a whole council of people like him."

Colleen, who sat to Marvin's left, laid a hand on his arm. "Listen to Jenna, dear. If our girl says it's better for you to stay behind, then we need to trust her."

"I just think it—I'd feel better if I could be there, that's all."

"Now, now, you'll do fine." Colleen gave his arm a few gentle pats of assurance. "We'll help you to keep your mind off things to make the time pass more quickly, won't we Patrick."

Patrick nodded agreement as Jenna called over to the table next to theirs. "And Tommy can take him to some movies to kill time, can't you?"

"Oh, absolutely. Dude, how long has it been since we took in a good flick? It's gotta be more than a month already." Tommy's expression turned dour for a moment. "Summer blockbuster season is really just heating up." His smile returned. "But I'm sure we can find a string of fun stuff."

"I don't want to talk about it, anymore. It's too depressing." Marvin dropped his sandwich and pushed away from the table, walked through the nearest wall to the outside and sat on the curb.

Jenna let loose an exasperated sigh and slammed her glass to the table. "Dammit."

When she moved to go after Marvin, Tommy stopped her. "No, I'll go." He walked through the wall, sat, and slung an arm around Marvin's slumped shoulders. "Dude, they're gonna be fine, you'll see."

Marvin gave him a wan smile. "I wish I had your level of confidence, hippie."

Chapter 31

Marvin slept soundly that night thanks to the almost-full bottle of wine Jenna had enticed him to drink. She had surreptitiously nursed a single glass to make him think she drank the same amount, and to make sure she wouldn't fall asleep.

Long before sunrise, Jenna pressed her body down through the mattress to slip out from under the arm and leg Marvin had flung over her, and dressed without a sound.

In the living room of the suite, she pulled the ever-present hotel stationary and pen from the drawer of the desk and wrote:

I know you don't understand it, but this is something I have to do. We'll do our best to make them—to convince Jason and the rest of the council we know what we're doing. It's...

She was going to write that it would all be fine but she didn't know for sure, no one did. It was entirely possible any member of this round table committee could stop them. All one needed to do was engulf them and swallow them up, sentencing them to an eternity of pain and darkness. A sudden violent shiver wracked her body and brought to mind the old childhood adage that someone had walked over her grave. Realizing she actually had a grave to walk over made her shiver again.

We'll be back soon. I love you, Marv, don't you ever forget that.

Jenna

She laid the note on the counter next to the coffee pot where he would see it as soon as he wandered out. Then she left to gather her cohorts.

Jenna figured that by the time Marvin found the note and slogged his way down the empty hallway to Mike and Tommy's suite at the opposite end of the building, she and the girls would probably be half way to Saulte Ste. Marie.

Chapter 32

"I'm sorry, Brody. But, it's probably a good thing they snuck out," Mike said, sipping on his coffee.

"I know." Marvin's pout didn't change. "But that doesn't mean I have to like it."

"No, dude, but you'll have to accept it." Tommy plopped onto the couch with his steaming mug. "Now, we just need to occupy ourselves until they get back. So, how's about we go hit the diner for breakfast, then we jump a bus to see a few movies, like Jenna suggested."

"How long do you think it'll take?"

"Mmm... Most movies these days seem to run well over two hours."

"That's not what I meant, ya schmuck, and you know it."

"Sorry, Marvin." Tommy rolled a finger at his temple. "The cobwebs haven't dissipated, yet."

"Look, Brody, there's no way we can anticipate it," Mike said, shrugging. "It could take a few days, it could be a few weeks. I mean, look how long it took them to convince Jason to put the issue to the full council."

"Mike, go snag a paper from the lobby, would you? So we can see what's playing?"

"It's over on the dining table already. Brody, grab it, could you?"

Marvin stood motionless at the window, just as he

did when Jenna still walked among the living. He had gazed out at the city skyline as if he could see through the intervening buildings, right into the condo, and watch over her every move. Now, he stared off in a northwest direction. He knew the island. It was the same one in the middle of Lake Superior Tommy and Mike had used more than a year ago to goad him out of his afterlife fantasy of killing Jenna. Though now it appeared the joke was on them all; as long as the North American Council of Keepers stood in residence, it really was where all the bad guys were kept.

"Brody!"

"What?"

"The paper?" Mike snapped his fingers.

"Yeah, yeah. Sheesh, give a guy a chance, would you?" Marvin grabbed the paper and held it out. "Who gets it?"

Tommy took it, went right to the listings, and a big smile spread across his face. "Now that will be a howl. That's it. Rave South 16."

Mike rolled his eyes. "I'm afraid to ask. What moldy musical are they showing now?"

Tommy's shoulders slumped, his lower lip protruded, and he feigned hurt feelings. "Mike, you cut me to the quick, man. I told you I was a sucker for a musical when you moved in."

"And I forgave you and stayed anyway. Imagine that." Mike winked.

"No, they snagged *Haunted 3D*." Tommy rattled the paper for effect.

"Seriously?" Marvin sighed. "You want to go see some ghost movie? Living it isn't good enough?"

"Living it." Tommy chuckled. "Man, that's funny.

Come on, just think of the fun we'll have. Dude, it'll be a real scream for us. In fact, I'll bet you dinner tonight the place will be full."

"What the hell, it's as good a way as any to pass the time."

"The first showing is at ten-forty-five. What time you got, Mike?"

"It's not quite eight-thirty."

Tommy looked up at the ceiling to do a quick calculation. "With the bus stops along the way, it'll take about forty minutes to get there. Cool, if we hurry, we have time for a leisurely breakfast."

"You mean time to mess with Tina," Mike corrected.

"Nah, she's no fun anymore." Tommy folded the paper and stood. "Shall we?"

"I hope to God you two plan on getting dressed first." Marvin gestured in the direction of a bedroom.

"Speaking of not any fun…" Mike flipped a bird at Marvin before following Tommy.

"Yeah, yeah, yeah." Marv laughed. "Whatever."

Thinking *Haunted 3D* wouldn't be Colleen's cup of tea, they only stopped to invite Davy and Dennis on the way out of the hotel. Moving through the door, Mike called out, "Hey, Davy, you here?"

"Just a sec." He emerged from the bathroom with a towel wrapped around his waist. "You need something, honey?"

"We're heading over to Epstein's for breakfast and then to see a movie. You two care to join us?"

"Oh, we've got a hundred things to attend to. Arrangements like this have to be made well in advance, you know. But it was sweet of you to ask."

Mike turned to leave but curiosity made him stop and ask, "Are you sure you're going to be able to pull this off? I don't mean to insult you or anything, but—"

"Oh, please." Davy waved off the slight. "Don't you worry. Honey, I'll relinquish my crown if this wedding doesn't come off as promised."

"Even at this grand scale?"

"Even at this grand scale."

"How can you be sure the cruise line won't interrupt everything?"

Davy laughed. "A woman I dressed for her funeral used to be a travel agent. She hacked their website, booked the yacht, and redlined the island for every schooner for two weeks. It's called Sandy Cay, by the way. Now, stop worrying about the wedding. Go. Enjoy your movie and let us do our work." Davy pushed Mike back through the door.

With a running time of one-hundred and forty-three minutes, the movie lasted longer than any of them had expected. Combined with the commercials and previews, the packed house of deadheads didn't filter out through the walls of the theater until almost two p.m.

"Holy mother of Mary, that was a long film." Marvin stretched to pop his back, and yawned. "Foreign, with captioning, no less. What was that, ten hours?"

"Dudes, if Jason had seen this, he'd be pissed at whoever is supposed to be policing India, let me tell you. And I wouldn't blame him a bit. What a crappy plot. That piano teacher turned out to be one mean, nasty, creepy guy. First he rapes his student, then after she kills him, he haunts the crap out of her until she commits suicide?"

"But that's exactly the kind of thing the girls are trying to prevent—rape and abuse—without the whole convoluted shenanigans of time travel that prevent the events, of course. I mean, what the hell was that all about?" Mike asked, trailing behind.

"That's what ruined the movie for me. Did you hear all the groans of disbelief in there? Sorry, dudes, I honestly thought we'd get more laughs out of it."

"So, now what?" Marv asked.

"Hey, whatever tickles your nuggets, Brody. This is all about keeping you happy, remember?" Mike poked him in the back.

"Yeah, well, what would tickle my nuggets would be following the girls to Michipicoten, and I'd be willing to bet that's not about to happen."

"We could pop in and watch *The Hangover II*," Tommy offered, reading the mini-marquees over the doors to each screening room. "Or, the new *Pirates of the Caribbean*. The first three were really good and you can't beat Johnny Depp. If you ask me, the guy is one of the most underappreciated actors of his time."

"Nobody asked, hippie."

"Et tu, Marvin? I swear, you two cut me to the quick and sever my un-beating heart." Tommy's voice feigned injury. He stood poised at the door to the *Pirates* movie. "Anyway, the best part about this one is, it's got even more dead people—and Captain Jack Sparrow is a total hoot. He's the funniest dead guy to come along since I can't remember when."

Chapter 33

Jason waited with nervous anticipation for the remainder of the thirteen members of the North American Council of Keepers to arrive and take their seats on the ground above the circle of stones that had been buried for centuries. With so much happening, weariness hung on him like the dark gray cloak that weighted down his slumping shoulders. He tried to breathe in a sense of calm from the fresh scent of the earth and send it in a wafting breeze over the group, like a healing balm. Though there were other meeting places like it scattered across the world, he'd chosen this meeting ground, the small meadow of Michipicoten Island in Lake Superior, because of the stillness it offered. Wildflowers with their bright white and pale yellow petals dotted the vale. Great green boughs hung as a canopy and swayed, allowing moonlight to flicker over the grass.

He looked up when stragglers from the farthest end of the continent rushed in and took their places at the edge of the wooded glen. "As the oldest of our kind, it fell on me to issue this summons." His deep cavernous voice rose above the rustle of the leaves. "It's been thousands of years since we've needed to convene and I may not have met every one of you. Let me take the time right now to thank you, not only for the response to my call, but for what you do. Without all of us, the world would be a very dark place." Pausing to adjust the cowl of his cloak provided the moment he needed to decide exactly how to begin. "This will be a discussion of protocol and circumstance. Conclusions tonight will be relayed to the World Council. I will need their approval before moving forward."

The woman seated in a line directly across the circle from Jason stood. "You look worn, Jason. Are you still capable?"

A male voice called out from her right. "Is that a challenge, Antonia?"

"No, not at all. I'm voicing concern. We all know, or at least *should* know, that there have been members far younger than Jason who have become too weary to continue."

Jason raised his hand for silence. "Antonia is observant. It's why a young protégé has been assigned to assist me. It's due to her that we meet."

Another voice carried across the glade. "Has she done something wrong?"

"Not wrong, no. She's…strayed from procedure and wishes us to adopt a new way of doing things. Perhaps it's best if I let her explain." With a small wave of his hand, Nancy stepped out of the shadows and stood beside him.

She looked from face to face, around the circle of cloaked figures who would one day become her peers. She clasped her hands to steady her nerves. "Jason sent me to observe an individual who passed suddenly, to measure his potential for harm. I understand those whose death is sudden can be difficult, and they sometimes pose the greatest challenge. As I reported to Jason, Marvin showed little penchant for real trouble.

But later he made a serious threat to the fiancée he'd left behind." She lowered her gaze to the ground and paused for a moment. "As Jason moved to take him, I intervened."

A chorus of gasps and murmurs only the dead could hear drifted across the expanse.

The representative from Eastern Canada stood and threw back the cowl of her cloak, which swirled with the suddenness of the motion. "You dared question the authority—"

The man who'd disputed Antonia's sincerity earlier now challenged Jason. "It appears she might be better suited to Teresa's sect, Jason. We can't have weakness among us; we can't allow evil to go free."

Nancy's head jerked up in surprise at the earnestness of the attack. "I apologize. I know it was wrong. But—"

"If you knew it was wrong, why did you do it? Is this man still wandering around unguarded?" he demanded.

Jason interrupted what threatened to become an inquisition. "Please! Let her continue."

Nancy raised her voice above the din. "I asked Jason to show him what would happen if he went through with killing his fiancée. Look, I know it's never been done before, but it seems to have worked. Marvin is a good man, his desire to kill was out of love and loneliness. Nothing more. If I'd been wrong, Jason would have completed his duty." Nancy looked to him for confirmation, and he nodded.

"Didn't that make him unstable?" a new voice inquired.

"It could have," Jason replied. "And it certainly

wouldn't work for all."

Yet another voice rose and demanded more details. "You're not telling us everything."

Jason looked directly at Nancy.

Nancy moved her gaze to the rustling leaves overhead. "I showed him."

"You showed him what?" Antonia asked in a soft, but strong voice.

"What he wanted would be delivered in time. He needed to be patient," Nancy explained in a low whisper.

Contentious grumbling rose from the group. One voice stood out among them and demanded punishment.

"We may know the when of the demise of the living, but we do not interfere! It's not allowed, Jason. You know this." The Keeper from southern Mexico pointed at him. "This cannot be allowed to continue."

Shouts of agreement echoed among the group until Jason again raised a hand for silence.

"She may be young," Jason said, nodding toward Nancy. "But, she's strong. I need her. My capacity, my strength to contain what I've gathered is weakening. The time will come soon when you will have to accept the distribution of my burden. It's difficult at best to find replacements. Her way may help us all to extend our time."

"What do we do when we've been deceived?" The Keeper from the northern regions of Mexico raised his arms with a sweeping gesture around the circle. "You know it can happen. How do you know this one, this Marvin, hasn't been clever enough to do so? If you're as close to your end, as tired and growing as weak as you say, can you tell us for certain he hasn't?"

Nancy placed a gentle touch to Jason's arm. "I've kept close watch on him. I will make the guarantee."

Jason sighed. "I didn't realize it would be this complicated to reach an agreement among us to at least try this new approach. I see that was in error. Then this discussion should be saved for another time." He slowly looked from one concerned and anxious expression to the next. "Right now, we face a far more serious issue."

"What could be more serious?" the young woman from Eastern Canada asked, and mumblings again swept across the glen in a flurry, like gatherings of fall leaves being scurried along by a dark wind.

Jason waited for the buzz to settle before he spoke again. "A boy has been killed and the perpetrator was not taken. This is—"

The circle of robed members' voices broke into a cacophony of queries. "Why?" "Who is the offender?" "How has this been allowed to happen?"

When the questions moved into the realm of accusations of collusion and finger pointing, Jason stepped forward, his voice booming with ultimate authority. "The boy's death was purely an accident, I can assure you, though he brought it upon himself by his own act of atrocity."

"Atrocity," spat out in disbelief.

Moving to the center of the conclave, Nancy stood in passive invitation. "Since you appear to question that, I can show you the boy if you like."

The Keepers of Mexico moved forward and a handful of others formed a line. The first locked eyes, his stature grew as he moved to engage Nancy. The moment his arms encircled her, Brandon leapt forward with hatred so black, the Keeper withdrew and shuddered. Returning to his spot on the perimeter, he announced with respect, "I hope you've got a solid grip on that one. I don't perceive a need for the rest of you to look, but see for yourselves if you must."

"Was it this Marvin you so vehemently defend that took the boy's life?" a new voice challenged as Nancy returned to her place beside Jason.

Nancy's shoulders straightened, ire remained in her voice. "No."

"Yet, why do I feel you had something to do with this, and that you're hiding something from us?"

"Perhaps, because I witnessed his death, though it shouldn't have happened the way it did, and now hold his evil at bay?" In a subtle movement, Jason placed a hand to Nancy's side to provide what little strength he could in his touch. She turned a subtle glance in his direction. He gave a slight nod of encouragement and permission. Nancy's voice rose with strength and a newly possessed authority. "Hiding something? I've got nothing to hide from you. Though I could relate the event, maybe you should hear it from the one who's responsible for his capture and subsequent safekeeping."

Jenna, Diane, Connie and Carla all stepped into the clearing to surprised whispers that echoed among the small open space, adding to the sounds of the quivering leaves above. Each stood with shoulders squared and head held high, and met the stunned but angry glare of each member of the Council.

"Is someone going to speak, or are you all going to stand there in silent defiance?"

The girls turned to Jenna, who rolled her shoulders as if to steady her nerves and then began. "I witnessed Brandon following a young girl. At some point he lured her behind the store and attacked her." The retelling of the scene renewed Jenna's anger and her voice became harsh and shrill. "He backhanded her, tore her blouse, and pinned her against the building. When I moved in, his—"

"You entered his body?"

"By mistake. To free her from his grip and lead her away. That's all I ever intended do when—"

The council members picked up on her words and spoke at once, talking over one another. The words snarled and hurled around the circle, voices rising to be heard. "You've done this before?—These women need to be dealt with, now.—It sounds as if she plans to continue, with or without permission.—What do you hope to accomplish, interfering in such a way?—It's becoming evident you hold a total disregard for our rules.—Jason, what do you intend to do?"

Connie and Carla cowered at the attack, and Diane froze. But, Jenna, unable to contain her emotions shouted, stunning the Council to silence. "Stop it. Do you want to know what happened or do you just want to make accusations?"

The opportunity to add strength to the truth of Jenna's statement made Nancy smile, and she interjected. "The boy was aware. When Jenna stumbled into him, he saw me. He threatened me."

Diane spoke up. "That's when I managed to get the girl to safety."

Jenna continued in her own defense. "I didn't intend to hurt him. My intent was to stop the attack.

That's all, plain and simple. He struggled to use me, I panicked trying to get free of him."

"What do you expect of us," Antonia asked.

"Permission to save lives," Jenna stated flatly.

"How?"

Jenna looked to Nancy and Jason who stood silent, waiting for an answer as much as the others. Diane spoke in her stead. "By getting victims to safety. We enter their bodies, and by leaving their attackers behind, help them escape. We take them to shelters where they can find the assistance they need. They don't know how they managed to escape, but they're appreciative of the help being offered."

A man to Jason's immediate right spoke for the first time. "Why should we concern ourselves with them in such a manner?"

Jenna opened her mouth to answer and Jason intervened. "The first time I came across Jenna getting involved, I stopped her. It took less than two weeks before the same man struck again. This time, the man died and the woman's life was saved. Yet, the whole second incident could've been avoided."

A confused and competing counterpoint chorus of debate sprang to life. Speculations of the positive and negative aspects shot across the circle in all directions. If asked, Jason would have voiced his approval of Jenna's intentions. Instead, he allowed the argument to rage on, expecting it to wear itself out before he could succeed. He closed his eyes, let his mind venture out until the one he sought answered his request. He smiled as she appeared.

Teresa's diminutive frame shimmered into view at the center of the circle, voices paused in mid-word, and an utter silence of awe and reverence fell upon the whole island. Living creatures halted; songbirds and owls stopped their calls; insects ceased their labors. An aura surrounded her body, a brilliant radiance glimmering from her aged countenance. Her smile never wavered. Turning from one face to another, her kind eyes invaded, digging deep into the members' minds, and calm settled over the circle. She clasped her hands in front of her, bowed her head for the briefest of curtsies toward Jason, and then spoke in a soft, assured voice.

"Jason's told me of your issue. I must say that any one of you who cannot see the innocence of the women standing here before you, understand their intention of good, has spent too many years on this council." She bent her gaze to a particular member. "You claim Nancy, and the rest of them," she said, motioning to the group of women still standing nearby in the center of the circle. "That they might be better suited for my work. I thank you for your suggestion, Marcus, but I hardly need help. I have no burdens. My charges are as light as the air, less than a grain of sand; each one at a peace you probably couldn't imagine.

"I know Jason agrees, though no one has asked for his opinion. If you would bother to think this through, you'd see that Jenna and her friends are helping you. Don't you understand that preventing evil things from happening is more effective than taking those who would perpetrate it? Perhaps, it's a step toward redemption?"

Teresa turned to him. "Jason, I don't need to consult with my members. As the Head of my Sect, Jenna, Diane, Carla and Connie, not only have my blessing to continue, they also have my permission to recruit others to their work. Since we agree, Jason, the World Council gives its consent. Though, if I'm right," she said, and gestured to Antonia, "you are about to lose at least one member of your sect to Jenna's new one."

Jason smiled and bowed to her.

Chapter 34

Not everyone was pleased, but not a single member of the sect dared to defy the wishes of the two most powerful Keepers. The figures that made up the circle, following Jason's lead, knelt in deep reverential bows. Moments later, when they rose, they discovered a small inner ring. Jenna stood with Teresa and Jason, their hands clasped and heads bowed. The three glimmered like celestial bodies. The entire glen brightened, but now the shadows of tree limbs danced upward from the light emanating from within the three.

"What are they doing?" Carla whispered.

Diane shook her head, but smiled. "I don't know, but my guess is that our girl is going to be very different when this is over."

The three heads slowly turned upward, the glow increasing in intensity, their necks craned backward until they faced the night sky, as if the power of the stars rained down and flowed into them. When they again faced each other and opened their eyes, the light that had once belonged only to Teresa, now shone in Jenna though it was less pronounced; a slight aura surrounded her. The fierce intelligence of Jason's gaze now inhabited hers.

Jason spoke, but his words were unintelligible to all but his two counterparts. To the others, the ancient language reverberated in a series of clicks. "You have accepted a position of authority and the Council welcomes you. You have been given power over others on our plane. I'll caution you to use great care. With the authority we give, you now bear a fearsome responsibility. Misuse them and they will be stripped from you."

They turned to face the others and Jason spoke again. "You are witness to the expansion of the World Council. Jenna now heads a new Sect. Her power is a combined ability; equal to mine, equal to Teresa's. Those who follow her shall be given authority to protect the living as she has done, as she instructs. Let your regions be made aware."

Teresa bowed her head and gave the slightest of curtsies. Jason acknowledged it with a small bow and the two figures dissipated. With their departure, the sounds of night returned to the island.

Chapter 35

"Holy mother of Mary!"

Marvin jumped from the couch and rushed toward Jenna so fast he plowed halfway through her before he stopped.

Four days after she'd snuck out, Jenna stood enduring Marvin's tight hugs and sighs of relief. "Marv, stop. Let go. I told you everything would work out. You just never trust me, do you?"

"I was worried, so sue me."

"Marvin, if I still worked for a law firm, I'd sue your ass for smothering me to death," Jenna said, breaking free with a laugh. "It's so late, I'm surprised you're still awake."

"So who could sleep?"

"Careful, there. You sound like your mother."

"Sorry." He backed away to arms' length and studied Jenna.

"What? I'm fine. See?" She did a slow spin for him.

"I see that, but something's different. I can't put my finger on it, but something is way different."

Jenna waved him off. "You're imagining things. How about a glass of that wine you stashed away a few weeks ago. Is there any left, or did you drink it all while I was gone?" She made her way to the balcony doors and paused. "Oh, and get enough glasses down for everyone. They'll be here in a couple of minutes."

Marvin couldn't quite figure out why but he didn't question her, and cast a quizzical glance in her direction before he set glasses out and opened three bottles of wine. He poured a glass for Jenna and grabbed his own from the coffee table on his way out to sit with her. "So, tell me. I want to hear everything. How did you convince Jason and the council, or whatever, to let you go? What did they say?"

Jenna reached over and took his hand and gazed out over the city for a moment. "When everyone gets here, I'll explain everything."

Beside Marvin's total relief, the reaction of the other men was mixed. Davy, busy with the increasingly detailed plans for the wedding, expressed his happiness that the hard work he'd already put in wouldn't go to waste.

Mike hugged her tight as he laughed. "See, Brody? All that worry, all that pacing around for nothing."

"Dude, that is so cool!" Tommy lurched around the room, chasing after everyone. "You guys will be like *Invasion of the Body Snatchers*."

****

It took months for Marvin to adjust to this new Jenna. She would leave at the oddest times with no explanation, she'd just be gone. When she returned, sometimes, to Marvin, she'd seem to carry a new burden; other times, there would be a smile on her face and he'd see a slight shimmering glow surrounding her. But the brightness she'd acquired in her green eyes on the trip to Michipicoten held firm.

Word spread quickly about the new sect of Keepers. They felt no need to remain in self-imposed shadows as Jason's members did. Though none could escape a direct command, Jason's sect preferred to blend into crowds to minimize their efforts.

When Jenna appeared anywhere, deadheads would smile in awe at the strength of conviction she displayed. The sect became inundated with applicants, though many didn't pass the test for various reasons. Either they couldn't grasp the ability to control the living without detection, or their motivation to be included was misplaced. Yet the number of members increased at a steady rate, fanning across continents. Jenna found herself deputizing (it was the only word she could think of) more and more men and women. With Nancy's increasing authority and help, Jenna appointed some to head regions and instilled them with the necessary power over the dead.

Though Jenna feared Marvin could detect the slightest edge of annoyance every so often, she no longer argued about the wedding, she only shook her head and said, "Are you sure you want to do this, Marv? I don't get it."

When the day came to leave for Sandy Cay, she calmly went along though she still hadn't agreed to marry him.

Chapter 36

Well past midnight, with the rest of his fellow travelers below deck in their cabins, Tommy stood alone at the bow of the "borrowed" schooner. In his usual attire, which was to say naked, he scanned the eastern shore of the tiny island they'd visited twice over the months since Marvin's death. The sails lowered and the ship slowed, and then dropped anchor. A sense of happiness settled over him; one he'd never known at any other moment of his life, alive or dead. He breathed in the fresh salt air and smiled.

He looked out over the small bay. A sailboat floated, moored a bit to the south, closer in to the sandy beach. Though the three-quarter moon had already passed to the west, thousands of stars made it so bright you could read a book. He squinted, trying to see the lettering on the stern, but he still couldn't make out the name. "Huh. And here we thought we'd have the place to ourselves for a day."

Not that it mattered since most of the living couldn't see or hear them. But, it wouldn't be more than another couple of days before the entire island would be surrounded by yachts and sailboats and schooners of all shapes and sizes, anchored in rows twenty deep, filled with deadheads from around the globe who'd be there to witness something that hadn't occurred in millennia, if ever. Even Jason couldn't remember a marriage between two deadheads taking place and he'd been around for more centuries than any of them could fathom.

Tommy had to admit, at first he didn't think it would happen. So many things had occurred over the past year to foil the plans; the biggest, of course, had been the trouble Jenna and Diane had stirred up. If that had turned out differently… He shivered at the thought. Then there had been Jenna's continued refusal to discuss even the smallest of details, which, after being summoned before the World Council of Keepers, turned to an odd sort of peaceful apathy. But, it appeared everything was in order. With his very own eyes, he'd seen the cotillion of organizers Davy had assembled and heard them confirm the plans one by one. In Davy's words, this indeed promised to be "An event."

Though there still was more than a sliver of doubt Jenna would go through with the wedding. Tommy shrugged and made his way to the hammock strung along the bow of the ship; his favorite place. He laid his head back and closed his eyes. The sound of the waves lapping against the side of the boat lulled him to sleep.

Hours later Tommy stretched the sleep from his body and spotted a young couple on the beach, hands shielding their eyes from the rising sun, as they peered out over the expanse of ocean to the small ship.

"Well, that's kind of weird, don't you think?" Evan's quiet voice matched the serenity of the light morning breeze which carried his words.

Vicky shrugged and nudged her companion with an elbow. "Why?"

"The cruise lines don't usually use this place

during off-season." The man dropped his hand and turned to the woman. "I'm sorry, honey. I really thought we'd have the place to ourselves. So much for having a honeymoon on our own tropic isle, huh?" he asked, heaving a mournful sigh.

"It's okay. I think the place is big enough we can still enjoy ourselves without being disturbed." Still watching, Vicky took a sudden, quick step backward. "Did you see that?"

Evan turned his face toward the schooner. "What?"

She pointed toward the bow. "There was a splash in the water. You know, like someone just dove in."

"Yeah, so?"

"But I didn't see anyone jump or anything. Do you see anyone out there?"

Evan took a few steps into the water. "You must be seeing things. Nobody's in the water." He adjusted the aim of his gaze. "There isn't even anyone on deck. Maybe it was a dolphin." With that, he turned and began walking along the edge of the water, his feet washed by the small waves rolling in.

Vicky alternated watching her new husband and peering out at the small schooner. A short while later she called out to him. "Uh, Evan...Evan! There's something creepy about that thing."

He'd barely made out her words, but he turned to the sound of her voice and called out. "Why? Honey, it's just a boat."

"Then why is one of the lifeboats being lowered into the water?"

"You think maybe because they're planning on bringing passengers out to the beach. What's the big deal, Vicky?"

"With nobody on it?" She brushed away a large hank of her brown hair that had blown into her face. "I don't like this. It doesn't feel right. Seriously, Ev, do you have your glasses?"

Evan pulled his glasses from their perpetual perch at the front of his shirt, put them on and stared out over the waves for a moment. "There's got to be someone in it. Boats don't row themselves. You just can't see them because the sun's glaring too much."

"Boats don't row without oars either, but this one is definitely moving this way." Vicky ran to his side and pulled on his arm. "Come on, let's go back to the tent."

"What for?"

"To pack up so we can get out of here!"

Evan turned her away from the water and wrapped his arms around her. "Vicky, honey, calm down, it's just a boat with people on it."

"Yeah, Vicky," Tommy stated, walking up out of the water. "We might be dead, but we're still people." Sea water ran from his long hair and dripped from the short pants he'd put on after Marvin had pestered him to no end during breakfast. He moved behind Evan and shook a hunk of seaweed from one foot. It landed on the beach with a wet splat.

To the living, water trickled from midair like some odd circular waterfall splashing to the wet sand. The seaweed put icing on the cake for Tommy when a visible chill ran down Vicky's spine. She opened her mouth and let out a blood-curdling scream.

Evan's eyes grew big behind the lenses of his glasses, his mouth gaped open like a fish desperate for the water.

The couple took off running to their tent, which stood under a copse of palm trees at the crest of the island. Jenna still stood in neck-high water because she hadn't wanted to add to the young girl's fright. "Tommy, that was just downright mean."

"Sorry, Jenna," Tommy said through laughter. "I couldn't help it. It's just that it's damn near impossible for me to pass up an opportunity like that. Besides, better to have them leave now than wake up tomorrow to an ocean of empty ships." He thought for a minute. "Well, empty to them, anyway."

Marvin swam up beside Jenna and then walked in purposeful strides to the shore where he smiled, winked and, for Jenna's benefit, smacked Tommy up through the backside of his head. "Ya schmuck."

"Dude…" Tommy grinned. "Ouch."

Marvin turned to gaze down the beach. "This was a great idea Davy had. I'm telling you, I could stay here forever. Where the hell is everyone?"

Tommy tapped his shoulder and pointed in the opposite direction at the nearing dinghy. "The spoilsports are landing."

Nancy, Mike, Dennis, Connie, Diane, and Carla clambered out, and Mike and Dennis pulled the boat up onto the sand to anchor it. They all turned when a duet of loud, frightened screams rose to unheard-of decibels. The group of deadheads stood and watched the mayhem.

Leaving the tent half disassembled, the couple grabbed a duffle bag each and ran, their feet barely disturbing the fine, white sand. They slung the bags overhead and waded to the small sailboat, tossed the bags on board, and scrambled up. Evan's shouted orders carried across the water. "Pull the anchor, pull the anchor."

"I'm trying. It's stuck on something!"

Evan pushed his wife out of the way, grabbed the crank and turned with all his might. The tautness popped loose and he slipped onto his backside.

Vicky reached down to help him up. "What happened, are you okay?"

Evan waved her off and shot a quick look toward the beach where trunks suddenly popped into view on the sand because Dennis and Mike claimed they'd already gotten bored with watching the fleeing couple. The man let out a resounding yelp. "Holy crap! Go raise the sail! Raise the sail!"

With the anchor up, and the sails rising and beginning to fill with the breeze, Evan disappeared into the small cabin. The sound of the engine trickled over the distance and, less than five minutes later, the deadheads watched the stern become a dot on the horizon as the boat headed out to sea.

Through it all Tommy had been doubled over in laughter. "And you thought I scared them with a tiny midair waterfall and a little kelp."

Chapter 37

Early the next morning, six small ships could be seen riding the gentle waves of the bay. Under Davy's strict instruction, their transport dinghies made trek after trek ferrying supplies to the leeward beach.

He ran over to a group of men in cargo shorts and t-shirts unloading a skiff. "What the hell are these? No, no, no! We've got to get the tents and canopy in place first." An exasperated sigh escaped and he poked a thumb over his shoulder. "Stack those chairs up on the crest."

Tommy, who had been awake for hours in excited anticipation, signaled to the men. "He means up here, guys," he hollered and headed down to the water's edge.

Davy turned to him. "Why can't anyone do anything right the first time? I swear I'm gonna have a heart attack and keel over before this is ready, and we just got started."

"Dude, that already happened." Tommy laughed and hugged him. "But it's going to be beautiful. Exactly what we wanted."

"You think? Oh, honey, I hope so. If these people would *stick to the plan I laid out for them*," Davy yelled, and waving his arms headed off to chastise another group.

The commotion of deadheads barking orders to one

another and the pounding of hammers to erect the canopies for the ceremony carried across the water to the schooner and woke the remainder of the wedding party. One by one they showed up and stood at the bow of the ship like a row of miscast mastheads. Sipping coffee, they watched Davy run from place to place, his flailing arms gestured wildly, pulled at his hair, and his shouted obscenities drifted out to sea.

Marvin raised his coffee mug toward the beach. "If he's not careful, there's going to be a mutiny."

"Well, why don't you go see if there's anything you can do to help?" Mike asked, leaning out over the rail past Carla and Connie, who stood between him and Marvin.

"Me? What could I do? I'm an advertising executive, not a wedding planner."

"Well, Brody, for once in your life, you could get sweaty and dirty. A little bit of physical labor isn't going to kill you, you know."

"Very funny, Mike. But, oh, hell no. Not me. One out-of-place petal on a flower and Davy would take my head off," Marv grunted. Tommy ran across the crest of the dune drawing Marvin's attention to his empty stomach. "What're we supposed to do for breakfast, if the hippie is over there?"

Mike chuckled. "Oh, for cryin' out loud, Brody, you never were capable of fending for yourself, were you? Tommy brought three dozen bagels from the deli; go stuff one in your craw."

Marvin's demeanor brightened considerably and a smile broke over his face. He turned to make his way to the stern and stopped. "Is there any cream cheese left? Can't have a bagel without a schmear."

Mike threw a friendly punch that swiped through Marvin's bicep and held out an empty mug. "Here, take this back to the galley, would you?"

Marvin took the cup. "Sure, I guess. You going somewhere?"

"Over there to see if I can help." Mike pulled his shirt off, dropped it to the deck, crawled up onto the rail and dove into the water.

By the time the sun went down that evening in a particularly spectacular flash of green on the windward side where they all stood, the island had been transformed. The trunk of every palm tree had been wrapped in tiny white lights. Waves crashing onto the sand muffled the low hum of generators that had been hidden in a copse of trees at the center of the speck of land.

In the gloaming, that time when day fades into twilight, outlines of the reception tents took on an eerie, otherworldly aura. Tiny bulbs on the corners and ridges glowed. The canvas walls had been pulled back to the corner posts like draperies revealing twenty-five round tables, each surrounded by ten chairs covered in white linen with sashes of teal and black satin. White silk table cloths were adorned with black runners, all secured by clear plastic clips. A single frosted globe light hung over each table, highlighting centerpieces of multi-colored Birds of Paradise. The platinum edges of the Limoges porcelain plates glimmered; silver and gold flatware and Waterford crystal glasses sparkled.

Almost all of the deadheads from the six ships stood in the sand next to an unusually quiet Davy, who stood with arms crossed, chin propped on his right fist the way it always was when studying his handiwork.

His brows knit and loosened as he made mental notes of what still needed to be tended to. He gave one short nod of approval and smiled. "Okay. I think we got a good start on things." He turned to a burly guy a few feet to his right. "Go ahead and kill the lights, Stephen."

Tommy pouted. "It's all so gorgeous. Do we have to?"

"Only if you want enough fuel to run everything for the event."

A collective, drawn out "Awwww" rose from the ghostly crowd when the generators shut down.

Mike called out to the group. "Come on, everyone, dinner has been laid out down on the beach over here. It's time to get this party started!"

"No drinking," Davy yelled as deadheads swarmed past him.

Tommy jabbed him with an elbow. "What?"

"Well…okay." Davy pointed an index finger at the backs of his workers. "But nobody better get drunk. I swear, if one—"

Tommy wrapped an arm around Davy's shoulder. "It's going to be perfect. Nothing could ruin this. After all, look who planned it."

"You think?" Davy thought for a moment then broke into a huge smile. "Yeah, you're right."

The two of them walked toward the bright sounds of reggae music emanating from the beach. Half way down the rise, Davy stopped and turned around to look at things one more time and grinned. "Yep. Di is going to wish I'd been alive to do hers."

Over the next two days, more and more guests arrived. The waters surrounding the island had become a sea of ships, from small four-berth sailboats to huge yachts. The America II, a four-mast ship out of Key West, stood out among the rest as the morning sun glistened off the gold trim and lettering of its gleaming black hull. Tongues wagged and engendered wagers about who might be on it. The captain, the only living soul aboard and not one to question orders to sail to this small island, anchor, and stay put for three days, laid out a selection of fine liquor at the bow to wait out the stay; in a drunken stupor, if need be, to stave off boredom.

"I don't care who it is," Davy stood under the wedding canopy and declared. "Nobody steps foot on this place until I say it's ready."

He looked out and studied his handiwork. At the very northern tip of the island he could see smoke rising from the vented top of the food tent, though the aroma couldn't tantalize him since it drifted eastward out to the open sea. The orchestra's bandstand, framed with stage lights, stood a bit higher on the incline. Because Davy had been told about the Judy Garland concert Tommy had taken Mike and Marvin to the previous year, the drummer's platform rose above the levels for the other musicians, and Davy hoped Marvin would be pleased and impressed with the surprise. In front of the bandstand were two pavilions large enough to accommodate one-hundred people on each of their dance floors. Stretching from those up to the canopy where he stood, and running the width of the island, were all the tents with tables for dining and relaxing. To the south, a four-foot-wide lighted path ran along the ridge line down to a beach on the leeward side where, since there was no father to give her away, Jenna would walk alone to the strains of a pre-recorded wedding march. That is, provided someone convinced her to do it. Guests fanned out across the sand would have to stand to watch; not that anyone grumbled. This was History being made; well, deadhead history, anyway.

Late in the afternoon as finishing touches were placed on the preparations, Davy caught sight of Versace arriving at the tiny south beach in a small launch and rushed down to help him disembark.

"The island is surrounded, it was quite the job maneuvering through them all," Gianni said, handing off Jenna's gown, and the tan linen bridesmaids dresses and tuxedos he'd instructed Davy find.

Davy's smile brightened. "I'd apologize, but I told you this was going to be big." He escorted the designer to a small tent where Jenna and her bridesmaids waited, and left to round up Marvin and the guys. Davy pointed to a small clearing. "Right over there, boys."

"What, no changing room?" Mike asked.

"Honey, if there's one thing you aren't, it's bashful. Now, I hope I can trust you to get into these by yourselves," Davy said, hurrying off back the way he came. By the time he parted the entrance to the women's dressing tent the sight took his breath away. Too stunned for flapping, his hands rose to his mouth in a delighted gasp.

"So, you must be pleased, yes?" Gianni gestured to the gown.

"Sweetie, you are gorgeous," Davy said to a grim-faced Jenna, and smiled at Versace. "I knew it. I knew you had to be the one to do this."

The bodice of the gown was made with a cream-colored silk. Jenna's auburn hair fell to her shoulders in flowing waves and glowed; her green eyes lit up, despite the dubious expression. The scooping cowl-style neckline, with threads of hand-stitched interwoven gold, draped from the tips of her shoulders and down across her breasts leaving ample cleavage, yet below her bosom it clung to her body. And, true to his word, Versace had designed the gathered-waist skirt so it draped in gentle folds that ended above the knee. The secret transformation to a wedding gown was in the undetectable overlay to the skirt. The hem matched in front and got longer as it cascaded to the back where it barely brushed the sand at her sandal clad feet, each fold a perfect match to the skirt. A five-foot long, delicate Italian lace train attached at her shoulders, held in place by a diamond encrusted gold chain, and a familiar-looking large blue sapphire surrounded by diamond baguettes dropped from her throat.

Jenna fingered the necklace and lifted her brows. "Well, I wonder where this came from."

"Oh, put a lid on it. Think of it as your something borrowed," came Diane's retort.

Tiny blue and white sapphires sparkled on the matching lace veil Nancy held.

Colleen wore a proud smile as she slipped the garter from her own wedding up to Jenna's thigh. "Oh, wait 'til Patrick sees you. His heart will melt. We're so happy and proud of you. You truly are the daughter we never had."

Jenna hugged her friend. "That's just too sweet of you."

Colleen gave a wave of her hand and smiled. "Oh, go on with you."

Placing his hands on Jenna's shoulders, Versace turned her around to face the full-length mirror leaning against the back of the tent. "You see, *bella*, you are the most stunning creature I have ever dressed."

Jenna quietly inspected her reflection, twisting left to right, and reacted with a brief smile.

Chapter 38

After inspecting every place setting on every table, checking on the progress of the food and drink, and ensuring everyone was ready, Davy nodded to himself in satisfaction. He placed tuxedoed greeters at various points to guide everyone to the south end and announced guests could begin disembarking. He stood on the leeward beach they'd used for staging everything to personally greet those arriving on that side of the island.

The last skiff to come ashore under his watch dropped from the America II and made him gasp in delight when he recognized its two passengers. *Oh, my God! Oh, my God! I could die!*

The captain, watching the small empty boat lower on its chains to the water on its own accord, mumbled that he was either drunk and overheated with sunstroke hallucinations or he wasn't quite drunk enough. Evidently deciding on the latter, he swigged heavily straight from a bottle of scotch.

Davy grabbed the bow of the skiff, thankful for being able to move without looking like an idiot, and pulled it as far up onto the sand as his strength allowed, then offered a hand to help the woman step down to the beach. Her short sandy blonde hair boasted a sparkling diamond tiara to match her necklace and earrings, the sky blue gown flowed down to her silver sandals, her smile radiating through blue eyes. Davy knelt on one knee, his excitement barely contained. "Your Highness."

Diana's lilting laugh carried across the beach. "Get up, silly! You must be Davy. There's no such thing as royalty here. That nonsense is strictly for the living." She noticed his eyes flit to the glint of jewels on her head and laughed again. "The tiara is just because…well, because I like it."

Davy stood, nodding like a simpleton, and tried to make actual words come out of this mouth, but failed.

Diana withdrew her hand and gestured to her companion, who had piloted the small craft to shore and stepped down to stand to her right. "I believe you know my friend, Dodi."

Davy's grin spread from ear to ear. "Pleased to meet you, sir. And, may I say what an honor it is to, that is, that you've come."

"We've heard so much about you, and about this event, that we couldn't possibly have missed it." Dodi extended a hand in greeting.

"Please, Your High—please, allow me to show you to the canopy area." Davy gestured in the correct direction. He followed, bouncing and waving his hands in the air, and squealing on the inside like a school girl who'd just been crowned Homecoming Queen. "Let me get some chairs for you."

"Absolutely not," Diana insisted. "We'll stand like everyone else."

****

Within an hour the entire south end of the island was swarming with chattering deadheads greeting one another, many who had never met. A Who's Who of the dead, stretching back more than a thousand years, had gathered from every corner of the world to stand witness to the world's first wedding of its kind. And Jenna had removed the overlay, train and veil, and dumped them all into Nancy's arms.

Jenna sighed and looked around at the people who'd made the trip. How so many dead folks had managed to "borrow" so much, from sailboats and clothes to enough jewels to fund a small nation, she couldn't quite fathom. Some she recognized from numerous films and television, and photos in celebrity magazines, others she couldn't place at all and shook her head in amazement.

"What is it, dear?" the woman next to her questioned.

"So many people…" Jenna replied, looking out at those who stood waist high in the water. Even more crowded along the rails of the boats moored as close as they dared without running aground, their perch providing better sightlines than many who stood on dry land.

"When I married Henry the streets surrounding the abbey were filled to capacity with cheering crowds on our wedding day. But, aren't you excited, so many people came to see you get married?"

Jenna's brows knit, and she looked across the beach to where Marvin stood sulking. Her reply came out confused and desultory. "I don't know…"

Eleanor turned a surprised gaze on Jenna. "You don't love him?"

"I do. But, I'm not so sure he loves me."

"Now, why would you say that?"

"Well, for starters, he tried to kill me."

Eleanor laughed. "Did he? Kill you, I mean?"

"No…."

Eleanor turned her gaze to a man standing closer to the pathway. "Henry wanted me beheaded."

"No! Really?"

"Oh, most certainly." She turned back to Jenna. "You see, we were fighting over which of our sons would inherit my land and his crown. He wanted me to die so he could marry someone younger to have more sons. Can you imagine? More sons to fight over. But, I knew he loved me when he locked me up in a convent instead. I got the last laugh and outlived him. When I finally drew my last breath, there he stood—waiting and smiling. Was Marvin waiting for you?"

"He was."

Eleanor lifted Jenna's chin and smiled at her. "Well, then…" she said with a questioning expression and tip of her head in Marvin's direction.

****

As Mike approached him, Marvin ceased muttering to himself. "I don't know why you all insisted on doing this. Look at her." He pointed to Jenna who stood at the opposite end of the beachhead. "She's not dressed. I told you she'd never go through with it. What a waste of money."

"What money, Brody? This hasn't cost any of us a single dime. Just relax, it won't go to waste, I promise. If nothing else, it'll be one hell of a party."

The lights twinkled on across the expanse, awed murmurs drowned out the hum of the generators as the sun dropped below the horizon, leaving behind a cerulean blue sky streaked with white and light gray clouds stained in shades of pink and red floating above the azure glass of the Caribbean.

Tommy came down from the wedding canopy, pushed his way between Mike and Marvin, and slung an arm over each of their shoulders. "It's gorgeous, don't you think? And the weather is perfect, warm with just the slightest breeze. A perfect day for a wedding, wouldn't you say?"

Marv growled. "Yeah, just perfect, if there was going to be one. I swear—"

Mike nudged Marvin, then turned to look at Tommy and smiled. "You look great. Doesn't he look great, Brody?"

"Yeah, yeah, great. All dressed up and nowhere to go."

"Aw, come on, Marv, lighten up. We're going to make history tonight, you'll see."

Still not convinced, Marvin stepped away and turned to look him over. "Well, hippie, I'll admit you clean up nice. Davy sure worked wonders with you. The tux fits like a glove. But if someone doesn't convince Jenna to do this, I'm afraid we've made this trip and Davy went through all this planning and work for nothing."

The speakers blared from the trunks of the palm trees to drown out Marvin's last few words. Mike wrapped his arm through Tommy's. "Are you ready to do this?" Tommy nodded. "Then let's get this thing started."

Arm in arm Mike and Tommy began up the path toward the wedding canopy. Marvin stood and glared at the unmoving Jenna. Tommy stopped and turned back to look at him. "Marvin! What are you doing? Come on, dude." Tommy motioned and held out a hand.

Marvin shrugged and went to them. With their arms linked and Marvin in the middle, the three made their way up the path. Teresa materialized and stood at the head, a shimmering glow surrounding her, her face lit with a smile. Though witnesses weren't exactly needed, considering there would be no marriage license or certificate, and come to think of it there was no judge or chaplain performing the ceremony since legalities here were a bit different, they pretty much set their own rules—well, the Council did, anyway—Davy and Patrick stood to the right; Diane, Connie, Carla, and Colleen on the left.

****

At the bottom, Jason appeared at Jenna's side. Nancy stood behind them with the overlay, train, and veil to her gown bundled carefully in her arms, waiting.

"This is nuts." Jenna turned to Nancy. "I've got too many responsibilities, now. Besides, eternity is an awful long time to spend with one person."

A young woman to Jenna's left laughed. "It may seem that, but turn it around. How long would it be without him?"

Jenna thought about the months she'd spent after Marvin's death, how long it had seemed, and how much she wished away the nagging that sent him scurrying out the door that morning right into the path of the bus.

"Nancy and I have enough faith in you to make up for your lack of it. You'll continue to carry out your duties, just as you've done for the past months. Now, come on," Jason said, holding his arm out for her.

Jenna took a deep breath. She turned and gestured to Nancy who wrapped and arranged the folds of the overlay, attached the train at Jenna's shoulders, and then draped the veil over her head and face. She kicked off her sandals, dug her toes into the warm sand, and hooked her arm to Jason's.

Walking up the aisle, heads turned, gasps and murmurs of appreciation among the guests grew louder as they moved past the crowd in hesitant steps. Jenna swore she noticed a few people actually bow and curtsy. She dared a peek upward. Tommy and Mike stood at Marvin's side, all smiles, waving her forward. Marvin's face beamed like any other bridegroom, and for a moment Jenna thought how silly it looked, how ridiculous all the pomp and circumstance was for a bunch of dead people.

At the top, Jason gave a deep bow to Teresa and joined the crowd.

Jenna turned to face Marvin. "Are you sure you want to do this?"

"More than anything I've ever wanted in my life."

"God, this is stupid. I mean, we're dead, who cares if we're married?"

Marvin took a sideway glance at Jenna's nervous smile. "I care. And I know you do, too."

Unsure, Jenna looked at him through the lace of her veil and saw the love reflected in the sparkle of his eyes. Her doubt melted away. The tentative smile turned to one of confidence, her green eyes lit with fun, and she poked a finger into his chest. "You know, Marv, eternity is a long time to spend putting up with your crap."

His eyes darted to see the most brilliant smile he'd ever witnessed on her. "You had this planned didn't you?"

"What?"

"This. You did it on purpose, didn't you?"

"What are you talking about, Marvin?"

"This whole time, making me believe you wouldn't go through with it, making me sweat. You enjoyed every minute of my misery, didn't you?"

"You know, Marv, you can be such an arrogant prick."

"And you can be a petulant bitch. Why don't you go fall down a flight of stairs."

"Oh…why don't you just go walk in front of bus."

Taking both her hands in his, Marvin winked. "For you? Anything."

A word about the author…

Paul Atreides turned writing for his own amusement into a career. A former theatre critic and columnist for Nevada's largest daily newspaper, he now reviews for EatMoreArtVegas.com.

He's had several short stories published in anthologies and is also a playwright. His two-act comedy-drama, "Phallusies," premiered in Las Vegas, Nevada, to good reviews, received Las Vegas City Life's "Pick of the Week," and most recently played to sold-out houses in Nashville, Tennessee. After submitting his ten-minute play, "Fusion," to the National September 11 Memorial & Museum in New York City he was invited to post it to the Artist's Registry in written form until filming can qualify it for installation as an exhibit within the museum.

He sits on the University of Nevada Las Vegas College of Fine Arts Advisory Board.

http://www.paul-atreides.com
https://twitter.com/atreides_paul
https://www.facebook.com/paul.atreides.391